Circus
PARADE

Jim Tully, 1886–1947

Circus
PARADE

By JIM TULLY

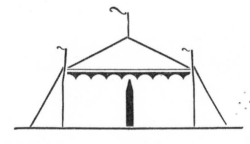

Illustrated by WILLIAM GROPPER

Edited by Paul J. Bauer and Mark Dawidziak
Foreword by Harvey Pekar

Black Squirrel Books
KENT, OHIO

© 2009 by The Kent State University Press, Kent, Ohio 44242
Library of Congress Catalog Card Number 2009000938
ISBN 978-1-60635-001-0
Manufactured in the United States of America

First published by Albert & Charles Boni, Inc., 1927.

Library of Congress Cataloging-in-Publication Data

Tully, Jim.
    Circus parade / by Jim Tully ; illustrated by William Gropper ;
edited by Paul Bauer and Mark Dawidziak ; foreword by
Harvey Pekar.
        p. cm.
    ISBN 978-1-60635-001-0 (pbk. : alk. paper) ∞
    I. Gropper, William, 1897–   II. Bauer, Paul, 1956–
III. Dawidziak, Mark, 1956–   IV. Title.
    PS3539.U44C57 2009
    813'.52—dc22   2009000938

British Library Cataloging-in-Publication data are available.
13 12 11 10 09   5 4 3 2 1

To

H. L. MENCKEN
GEORGE JEAN NATHAN
DONALD FREEMAN
JAMES CRUZE
and
FREDERICK PALMER
CIVILIZED COMRADES
IN THE
CIRCUS OF LIFE

Contents

[vii]

Foreword

Harvey Pekar

Jim Tully was one of the fine American novelists to emerge in the 1920s and '30s. He gained this position with intelligence, sensitivity, and hard work. Born in St. Marys, Ohio, in 1886 to Irish parents, Tully was placed in an orphanage at the age of six when his mother died. He ran away at eleven, working as a farmhand and then becoming a hobo until age twenty-one. Despite his troubled childhood, he managed to give himself a good literary education. He haunted libraries and read Balzac, Dostoyevsky, Gorky, Twain, and his early idol, Jack London, among others.

After working as a newspaper reporter in Akron, Tully settled in Hollywood and worked for a time as a press agent for Charlie Chaplin. He wrote or cowrote more than two dozen volumes, not all of them published, until his death in 1947. By that time, his work had gained the praise of H. L. Mencken and George Jean Nathan.

Published in 1927, *Circus Parade* deals with the time Tully worked as a laborer for a traveling circus. He did this because the state of Mississippi, where he was located, treated hoboes so badly. "In other parts of the United

Foreword

States a tramp is not molested if he keeps off railroad property," Tully wrote in *Circus Parade*. In Mississippi, however, a price is put on his head. With no money to pay the vagrancy fine, he is put to work at twenty-five cents a day and can spend several years as a virtual slave of the state.

Circus Parade consists of a series of vignettes, rather than a tight narrative structure. The first chapter, for example, has to do with a black lion tamer. Tully notes that most lion tamers he's encountered have been black. In *Circus Parade* and in other books, Tully pays special attention to blacks. He sympathizes with them, although he also seems puzzled by them. Anybody who loved the Irish as much as Tully might have a hard time fully understanding another minority group, but Tully was the exception. Consider his attitude in *Blood on the Moon* (1931) toward Joe Gans, the great African American lightweight boxer of the early twentieth century. Gans was obviously a bright guy with a good sense of humor. He wasn't easy for Tully to categorize. Tully wrote, "His features were more Semitic than Negroid" and "if the art of pugilism can reach genius, Gans was so gifted. The elements were blended in him—stamina, caution, cunning, swift and terrible execution." *Blood on the Moon* joins *Circus Parade* as one of Tully's finest achievements.

Circus Parade contains some of Tully's most memorable characters, black and white. The book differs from his

Foreword

other autobiographical works as the plot revolves around other circus employees, not himself. For example, the owner of the circus was a seventy-three-year-old carny veteran named Cameron, a clever con artist who was extremely cheap. Cameron was not well liked by most of his employees. Nonetheless, they all stuck together when they were attacked. Their rallying cry was "Hey, Rube!" as they hurried to fight oil workers or townspeople or anyone looking for a fight.

Tully also writes about people in the side show, like "The Moss-Haired Girl," a beautiful young woman who dyed her hair green and was the object of wonder to many customers. Another circus attraction was Lila, the four-hundred-pound German strong woman. She was a stellar attraction, but then she started buying fashionable clothes and reading romance novels. Her desire for a man led to tragic results.

I wondered if Tully had actually known Lila, or whatever her name was. But the important thing is that he made her and the scene believable, both with his economical, straightforward, no-nonsense writing style and his inclusion of many details that give the whole story the air of truth. He does this often. No matter how crazily violent or fantastic his stories are, you accept them as nonfiction. Tully makes the improbable seem true. But then he must have had some amazing experiences in his hobo years. He was even a prizefighter for a time.

Foreword

Where does Tully fit among the writers of his time? His work was relatively popular and received much critical praise during his lifetime. He created an original style, blending a spare writing approach with some fantastic stories, often about lower-class life with slang dialects and phonetic spellings (he had a very good ear). Tully was somewhat anticipated by Stephen Crane in tone, however, particularly in *Maggie: A Girl of the Streets* (1893). Crane wrote about life in the New York City slums, using slang and phonetic spelling: "'Run, Jimmie, run! Dey'll get yehs,' screamed a retreating Rum Alley child. 'Naw,' responded Jimmie with a valiant roar, 'dese Micks can't make me run.'" I can find no evidence that Tully ever read Crane or was influenced by him; the similarities could very well be coincidental. But Crane, who died in 1900, obviously anticipated Tully, whose first novel was published in 1922. Tully read so much that a number of writers probably influenced his style, whether he realized it or not.

Regarding Tully's huge appetite for literature of all kinds, it's interesting to note that he had a real respect for at least some avant-garde writing, as his sensitive and perceptive chapter on James Joyce in *Beggars Abroad* illustrates. The fiction-reading public these days is about as confused about Joyce as it was when *Ulysses* was published.

As for Tully's legacy, perhaps it is most clearly seen in detective stories beginning about 1930. His work often had

Foreword

a tough quality, but it is genuine, not affected like Ernest Hemingway's.

The Kent State University Press should be praised for publishing long-out-of-print works by this important Ohio writer. I hope we will see a renewal of interest in his work and additional volumes published, including Tully's writing about Hollywood. He wrote an early novel about the film industry (*Jarnegan*, 1926), an unpublished biography of Charlie Chaplin, and many uncollected movie articles for magazines and newspapers.

In one interview, Tully claimed he had "the best library in Hollywood." I believe it.

Introduction
Paul J. Bauer and Mark Dawidziak

Jim Tully (June 3, 1886–June 22, 1947) was an American writer who won critical acclaim and commercial success in the 1920s and '30s. His rags-to-riches career may qualify him as the greatest long shot in American literature. Born near St. Marys, Ohio, to an Irish immigrant ditch-digger and his wife, Tully enjoyed a relatively happy but impoverished childhood until the death of his mother in 1892. Unable to care for him, his father sent him to an orphanage in Cincinnati. He remained there for six lonely and miserable years. What further education he acquired came in the hobo camps, boxcars, railroad yards, and public libraries scattered across the country. Finally, weary of the road, he arrived in Kent, Ohio, where he worked as a chainmaker, professional boxer, and tree surgeon. He also began to write, mostly poetry, which was published in the area newspapers.

Tully moved to Hollywood in 1912, when he began writing in earnest. His literary career took two distinct paths. He became one of the first reporters to cover Hollywood. As a freelancer, he was not constrained by the studios and wrote about Hollywood celebrities (including Charlie

Introduction

Chaplin, for whom he had worked) in ways that they did not always find agreeable. For these pieces, rather tame by current standards, he became known as the most-feared man in Hollywood—a title he relished. Less lucrative, but closer to his heart, were the dark novels he wrote about his life on the road and the American underclass. He also wrote an affectionate memoir of his childhood with his extended Irish family, as well as novels on prostitution, boxing, Hollywood, and a travel book. While some of the more graphic books ran afoul of the censors, they were also embraced by critics, including H. L. Mencken, George Jean Nathan, and Rupert Hughes. Tully, Hughes wrote, "has fathered the school of hard-boiled writing so zealously cultivated by Ernest Hemingway and lesser luminaries."

Circus Parade, completed in March 1927 and published that summer, was Jim Tully's fourth book. After the Hollywood novel, *Jarnegan* (1926), he returned to his memories of the road. In many ways, *Circus Parade* may be viewed as a sequel to *Beggars of Life,* his 1924 bestseller about his years as a road kid. Indeed, they became the first two volumes in what Tully later called his underworld books.

Drawing on his own time as a circus roustabout, Tully's first story of circus life appeared in *Vanity Fair* in 1925 with chapters from what would become *Circus Parade* appearing in 1926 in *Liberty* and later in *Vanity Fair.* Introductory

Introduction

blurbs on the dust jacket were provided by Harry Hansen ("the small town circus as it was, in straight-hitting fashion") and William Allen White ("hard, terrible realism that will shock the life out of unsophisticated readers"). Early Tully booster George Jean Nathan was especially enthusiastic: "Tully has got the rawness of life as few American writers have been able to get it, and, with it, a share of poetry and of very shrewd perception . . . a view of mortals and of their sawdust hearts that will not soon vanish from the memory."

Tully dedicated *Circus Parade* to Nathan and Mencken, editors of *The American Mercury,* Donald Freeman, managing editor of *Vanity Fair,* and Tully's Hollywood pals James Cruze and Frederick Palmer. Mencken's editorial contributions went beyond friendship, and Tully inscribed the Sage of Baltimore's copy: "To H. L. Mencken with high appreciation to one who made the book possible."

If Tully appreciated Mencken's assistance, Mencken certainly appreciated Tully's hard-edged, straightforward style.

Some writers, like musicians, seem to write to an internal metronome. Tully wrote to the click-clack-click-clack of the rails, which became the unadorned, crisp, staccato rhythm of his prose. And like the view from an open boxcar, *Circus Parade* consists of a series of vignettes, each flashing by without reflection or rumination before the next scene is in front of the reader.

The narrator of *Circus Parade* is as memorable as his

Introduction

counterpart in *Beggars of Life*, but while *Beggars of Life* is a panorama of great memories, *Circus Parade* is a panorama of great characters. And those characters populate the tents and wagons of an outfit grandly billed as Cameron's World's Greatest Combined Shows. Despite the name, no one would confuse Cameron's ten-car collection of carnies, freaks, and other sawdust celebrities with The Greatest Show on Earth.

The characters that populate *Circus Parade* range from the sympathetic and innocent through the merely distasteful and cold-hearted to the cruel and black-hearted. The carnies include:

- Bob Cameron, the troupe's "sardonic and brutal" owner
- his wife, a greedy crone affectionately known as "the baby buzzard"
- John Quincy Adams, the guileless black clown who performs in whiteface
- the Moss-Haired Girl, a sideshow attraction so named for her green hair and based in part on an Irish-Indian girl Tully had once loved
- Slug Finnerty, the one-eyed barker or "spieler" who'd done time in the penitentiary for the rape of a young boy and was "the leader of the gang of crooks"
- Lila, the kind-hearted, lonely, 400-pound "Strong Woman" who whiles away her nights reading romance novels
- Blackie, amoral and bestial, a roustabout, heroin addict

Introduction

The boyhood dream to run away with the circus ran deep in the American psyche. "When a circus came and went," wrote Mark Twain in *Life on the Mississippi* (1883), "it left us all burning to become clowns."

Looking at the lions in their cages, Tully is struck by his own sense of freedom. His gaze shifts to the crawlers— legless men strapped to small, wheeled platforms who moan with pain to boost their take from the crowd. It is a clear message. Tully has not set out to write a romantic story of a boy joining the circus. He knows too well its seamier side. *Circus Parade* is as far removed from *Toby Tyler* as *The Maltese Falcon* is from *The Hardy Boys*.

Instead, over the course of the book, Tully paints a picture of life at the edges—earthy, wolfish, and brutal. "A circus is, or was," Tully writes, "generally a canvas nest of petty thieves and criminals among the lower gentry." The lambs among them repeatedly fall to the predators.

While good and evil play out in *Circus Parade*, Tully is not especially interested in questions of morality and immorality. Rather, he is fascinated by amorality. Tully makes a distinction between the amoral Blackie and the greedy and immoral circus bosses. Tully's character passes one rainy night playing cards with other roustabouts when Blackie stands up, pulls a gun, and robs them. Then, in grand pirate tradition, Blackie "red-lights" the men, forcing them to jump from the moving train. Tully's character falls back on his hobo instincts, scrambles to his feet,

Introduction

catches the last car, and pulls himself back on-board. He has no interest in revenge. "I had no love for the red-lighted men. Rather, I admired Blackie more. Neither did I blame him for red-lighting me. A man had once trusted another in my world. He was betrayed."

Blackie lived by a code. It may have been nothing more than the basic code of the animal to survive, but it was honest and without pretense. Just survive.

With *Circus Parade,* Tully's dreams of popular and critical acceptance were met. Sales were strong, the Literary Guild quickly contracted for a 16,000-copy reprint, Hollywood sought the film rights, and the comments from friends and formal reviews were strong, even ecstatic. One reviewer noted that the book was not for those "easily shocked." "But," he continued, "there is something other than bare naturalism in this book, a glowing overtone of humanity, comprehension, and pity that cannot be too highly prized."

A teenage James Agee wrote that *Circus Parade* was "remarkable chiefly for its nakedness of style, and for uncovering the most abysmal brutality I've even imagined could exist." The Harlem Renaissance poet Countee Cullen took note of the book's several black characters. "This book," he wrote, "will destroy some illusions, but that is the natural function of truth." And years later, Langston Hughes wrote Tully that he was on his third reading of the book.

There were, predictably, naysayers. Father Francis Finn,

Introduction

S.J., who recalled Jim as a scullery boy at St. Xavier's College in Cincinnati, recognized Tully's literary talents but decried what he saw as Tully's paganism and gloom. He further found Tully's work "offensive to Christian modesty" for which he blamed the bad company of hoboes in general and Charlie Chaplin in particular.

Critics found the chapter in which a young black girl is mercilessly degraded especially outrageous. Tully later noted that he recalled the incident from his circus days and put it to paper with little embellishment.

Adding to the furor, the Brooklyn Public Library prohibited its copy from circulating. A library in Idaho, according to one Tully correspondent, circulated the novel but with the offending chapter ripped from the book. And in Boston, the Watch and Ward Society declared an outright ban. *Circus Parade* joined a Watch and Ward list of banned books that included Sherwood Anderson's *Dark Laughter,* William Faulkner's *Mosquitoes,* Theodore Dreiser's *An American Tragedy,* Sinclair Lewis's *Elmer Gantry,* and Hemingway's *The Sun Also Rises.*

In a letter to H. L. Mencken, whose *American Mercury* had run afoul of Boston's Watch and Ward Society the previous year, Tully joked that he planned to go to Boston and pass out copies of the book to the hoboes, as they were "the only cultivated men I could find in the city."

While Tully could laugh off criticism from Boston, a bad review from St. Marys stung. Tully's hometown news-

Introduction

paper, the *Evening Leader,* in an editorial titled "Filth in Books," claimed to be "unpleasantly surprised that so much dirt could be packed between the covers of a book." In the view of the *Evening Leader,* "*Circus Parade* was written without excuse, except perhaps of making money." While acknowledging that Tully was a "clever writer" and "knows of what he writes," the newspaper could see no justification for exposing the public to such sordid subject matter. Tully's hometown paper widened its condemnation to include *Beggars of Life* and *Jarnegan,* advocating that the publication of all such books be prohibited.

Hurt and angered by criticism from home, Tully responded in a letter to the editor published in October 1927. Tully cited Mencken's comparison of him to Gorky and noted he and the great Russian writer of the underclass have something else in common: both come from hometowns ashamed of them. Clearly old wounds had been opened. "When I was a hungry boy in St. Marys," he wrote, "I got no understanding. I am getting none now." If his goal was getting rich, he argued, then he might adopt the maudlin style of the then-popular novelist Harold Bell Wright. Instead, "I write the truth." Had he taken his own counsel, he might have stopped there, but some bridges were made to be burned. In words that soured relations with many in his hometown for the rest of his life, Tully noted that "St. Marys is still in the same mental rut that it was in when I had the sadness of living there." Nor would

[xxii]

Introduction

he deal in the "childish terms of small Ohio towns." The sarcasm of the paper's response dripped off the page. "Jim, you are great. Wonderful! You and Gorky!"

Not content to get the last word but once, the *Evening Leader* returned to the subject of its famous native son in November by noting and reprinting the poor review of *Circus Parade* that appeared in a South Bend paper. The central criticism of the Indiana review—that *Circus Parade* presented an inaccurate picture of circus life—echoed the view of Eugene Whitmore in *The Bookman*. While acknowledging that *Circus Parade* had been "hailed by dozens of critics as a masterpiece of realistic writing," Whitmore charged that the book was "no more than old-fashioned melodrama, minus the lily-white hero and heroine." And, Whitmore continued, "Tully paints in dark colors, with no lightening contrasts."

On the first point, Whitmore was half-right. There are no heroes in *Circus Parade,* but a hero's struggle is an essential element of melodrama. Whatever *Circus Parade* was, it wasn't "old-fashioned melodrama." On the second point, there can be no argument. Tully did paint in "dark colors." If Whitmore had come to the book for sweetness and light, he had come to the wrong place and the wrong writer.

In building his case that *Circus Parade* was not realistic, Whitmore relied on what he saw as factual errors about circus life. He chided Tully for faulty geography, quoting

Introduction

Tully for writing, "we traveled as far inland as Beaumont, Texas," when, in fact, Beaumont is a port town on the Gulf of Mexico. Tully's meaning of westward travel is clear, however, when he is correctly quoted: "We had journeyed along the Gulf of Mexico and as far inland as Beaumont, Texas."

Whitmore, who claimed "a lifetime of contact with circuses," also objected to "Tully's ignorance of the nomenclature of circus tents," the description of loading and unloading the circus train, the troupe's travel in the south before the "cotton has been picked and marketed," and, in his view, other implausibilities and misstatements of fact. Clearly, *Circus Parade* was not to the liking of old circus men.

James Stevens, whose acclaimed novel about Paul Bunyan and lumber camps had appeared in 1925, wrote Burton Rascoe, the editor of *The Bookman*, to protest Whitmore's attack on *Circus Parade*. Twain's nonfiction *Life on the Mississippi*, he noted, was roundly denounced by "old steamboat men," and lawyers quibbled with Dreiser's *An American Tragedy*. A novelist, Stevens argued, is certainly allowed to sacrifice "fact for effect."

For his part, Tully dismissed Whitmore as a circus press agent. And, if some of the book seemed unbelievable, he had in fact excluded some memories that readers might have found too far-fetched. Tully wrote H. L. Mencken that he had omitted as unbelievable the tale of a drunk

Introduction

emerging unhurt from a lion's cage after flopping there for the night, even though he had witnessed it.

Circus fans and apologists would not yield. The Literary Guild received many cancellations over its selection of the book and, when it appeared in 1929 that a film version of *Circus Parade* would be produced, the Circus Fans Association mounted a vigorous publicity campaign opposing the movie. The *Circus Parade* movie was never made. A gritty portrayal of the big top would finally reach the big screen in 1932. It was *Dracula* director Tod Browning's *Freaks,* and it too was roundly condemned, even banned. More than seventy years later, *Freaks* is a cult classic.

Circus Parade would not be the last time that Tully ended up in the gun sights of censors and other self-appointed guardians of public taste and morality. In an odd footnote to *Circus Parade* and censorship, John O'Hara defended his use of the word "nookey" in a story he submitted to *The New Yorker* in 1960. If Jim Tully could use "goosey" in *Circus Parade,* O'Hara argued to William Maxwell, then "nookey" should be allowed to stand.

In *Beggars of Life,* Jim Tully found his voice: raw, powerful, savage yet lyrical. In *Circus Parade* that voice reached full-throated maturity: still savage, yet more confident in its ability to guide the reader down dark roads.

I: The Lion Tamer

I: The Lion Tamer

I T was my second hobo journey through Mississippi. After the first I had vowed never to return, but Arkansas moonshine had changed my plans. Three times the first week I narrowly escaped arrest. Then hurrying toward Louisiana, I lost track of the days of the week and month. There was no need to know. I had, as the hoboes say, dragged a long haul from Hot Springs, Arkansas, to McComb City, Mississippi, some hundreds of miles. The latter town is a sun-scorched group of frame houses stretched forlornly along the Illinois Central tracks, ninety miles from New Orleans.

Half dazed from loss of sleep, weak from hunger, and irritated by vermin-infested clothes, I resolved to leave the road for a spell. The terrible Mississippi vagrancy law hung over me. Under that law an officer is given two dollars and a half for every vagrant he captures alive. In other parts of the United States a tramp is not molested if he keeps off railroad property, but in Mississippi he is hunted up hill and down dale for the two dollars and fifty cents.

[3]

Circus Parade

Once captured, he is given a fine of seventy-five dollars. Having no money, he is made to work the fine out—at twenty cents a day! This comes to about eleven months and twenty-nine days, allowing a few days for good behavior. But there is, furthermore, a joker. The prisoner always needs clothing. He is charged three dollars for a fifty-cent pair of overalls, and seven dollars for a pair of dollar-and-a-quarter brogans. These debts are added to his sentence and worked out at twenty cents a day. It is no uncommon thing for a friendless man to spend several years as a peon in Mississippi. So I had reason to worry.

Life had been completely against me for weeks. I had, with the sincerest motives, left Hot Springs for the remoter Arkansas wilds with a pair of loaded dice in my pocket. I hoped to trade my virtuosity with them for the money which the blasé lumberjacks had taken from the Lumber Interests. With this end in view I had actually worked two weeks at a camp near Pine Bluff. When pay-day came I started a crap game on the stump of an immense pine tree. To my befuddled consternation I lost every dime I had. And I had worked so hard for the money! Trekking wearily back to camp after the game, I felt sure that someone had cheated, but not

[4]

The Lion Tamer

wishing to accuse anyone unjustly, I kept still. The Jewish manager of the company store had played.

It was my intention to beg a few dollars and leave the camp next morning. But a cyclone, speeding hundreds of miles an hour, roared across the State. It broke large trees as though they were toothpicks in the hands of traveling salesmen. It was a swirling funnel of doom. It sounded like the agitated rumbling of thousands of locomotives climbing a steep hill. We hurried to the cyclone cellars dug deep in the ground. The landscape next morning was as clean as a desert bone. I was drafted into the army of labor again. On my next pay-day I started another crap game in which the Jewish storekeeper played. I lost again.

Downcast, I left Pine Bluff and finally reached McComb City. Not wishing to bother the police with my presence, I circled the town. Five miles beyond it I walked toward the railroad tracks again. I waited on a grade which freight trains would climb slowly. In about an hour a coatless Negro wearing a black satin shirt limped along the track. He whistled *My country, 'tis of thee.*

"Which way, Patriot?" I yelled.

"Lawdy, boy—you sure skeert me. I done thought you was the law!" He laughed. "I'se on my way,

Circus Parade

brotheh, out of Mississip to Luziana. An bulieve me, boy, dey t'rows de key 'way on you when dey gets you heah. You bettah walk along wit' me—I'se headed south. Dey's a circus oveh in Baton—an' I'm a-trailin' it."

Lonely, I joined the Negro and headed for Louisiana. He was a beggar who followed crowds—a professional trailer. When we reached New Orleans, he fell into the train of an evangelist who was packing a tabernacle in the city. I went on to Baton Rouge and the circus.

The ringmaster gave me a job helping take care of the animals. My duties were light, and my sense of freedom was enhanced by seeing the animals behind the bars. The man under whom I worked was known as the lion tamer. He helped me get clean clothing and new shoes. It was fully a week before I recovered from the punishment of the road. I soon realized that my Negro acquaintance had been wise in not trailing that circus. It already had too many trailers following it.

Trailers are men who follow circuses or anything else that draws a crowd. They live by preying upon the people. Among the trailers with this circus were legless men called crawlers, who traveled with their bodies strapped to small wheeled platforms.

[6]

The Lion Tamer

They propelled themselves with stirrups held in each hand. They literally walked with their hands. Each time they struck the ground with a stirrup the wheels rolled under them. There were, too, trailers born double-jointed, who twisted their bodies in every conceivable and grotesque manner. Hard faces they had, and they moaned with pain when anyone drew near who might give money. Other trailers there were who could play the part of blind men. Yet others knew how to twist their hands.

One trailer carried a hard slice of bread with him. He would drop it on the sidewalk at a convenient place. When he saw a person approaching he would dive madly for the bread. This trick seldom failed to reap its reward. Another old trailer was a particular pet of the lion tamer's. I soon became attached to him also. He walked about, playing blind, tapping a crooked gnarled cane on the pavement. He would tap three times every ten or twelve feet. He wore a long tobacco-stained beard that reached to his belt. The whiskers hid all of his face but the eyes, over which his brows projected at least an inch. He belonged to the great body of men who write. As may be supposed he was not always tolerant of other literati. Since his doggerel rhymed,

[7]

Circus Parade

he had a special scorn for writers of blank verse.

"Them guys don't say nothin' an' what they do say they don't make no rhyme. They hain't artists," was the way he dismissed them. "Besides, they hain't no money in blank verse. People don't buy it. A fellow's got to sell his stuff if he wants to eat. I wrote a lot o' that damn blank verse one time, an' I had to give it to a barber for a haircut. He used it for shavin' paper. He's just got through usin' a swell big book of Shakespeare. Some critic give it to him."

This literary vagabond sold his own efforts for as low as ten cents a sheet. Playing the rôle of a neglected genius, he often begged large sums of money at the Southern colleges.

The lion tamer was the king of our small world. He was a lithe, two hundred pound Negro. Twice a day he went into a cage with six lions. Three of them were vicious and had killed several men. The strain of appearing with them told on his nerves. He kept up his courage with liquor.

Save for helping me to obtain clothes and shoes, he did not unbend to me until we had journeyed along the Gulf of Mexico and as far inland as Beaumont, Texas. The circus was pitched near some oil wells in Beaumont. I told the lion tamer

[8]

The Lion Tamer

something of the history of oil; I was from an oil section of Ohio. He was fascinated by the way wells were shot and the oil obtained. When I told him how nitro-glycerine was sent hundreds of feet into the earth and then exploded, and described the rush of the oil upward, he listened as though it were a fairy tale.

From that day on we were close friends. Every trailer and flunky with the circus, it appeared, had told him a fascinating tale at some time or another. He was everybody's friend. And yet his face was defiance carved in ebony. The more he drank the more it became stern and set. He never smiled. But he gave a great deal of his salary to the poor trailers.

He was quick of movement and about six feet tall. He carried a musical instrument with him that was neither mandolin nor guitar. It was a contraption he had made himself. Often, when the show was over, he would evoke from that instrument the weirdest music in the world. I used to watch him as he played. The dim light would reveal his face, as drawn as a long-trained bruiser's. His music had a soothing effect on the animals, especially the lions. He would sit very still and play late into the night. The more he drank, the more weird his music became. No one ever complained.

Circus Parade

A little ex-jockey, in charge of the horses, would often come and listen. We would seldom talk. Now and then an animal would make a moaning noise. Once the old Homeric trailer went suddenly dotty for an instant and screamed aloud. The lion tamer soothed him. The next day he wrote another poem.

One night the old trailer, the ex-jockey, the lion tamer and myself talked about death.

"I never worry about dying," said the lion tamer, "when the Big Guy yells my name I'll go—that's all."

Just the same he would drink heavily before entering the cages with the animals. Curious as to how he managed to control them, I asked him the secret.

"It's nothing," he said. "You must always look an animal in the eye. They can tell by that how game you are. You never can fool them."

About three hundred miles from Beaumont a crowd gathered in front of a cage which contained two laughing hyenas and a brown bear. The bear was blind. It had lost its sight in a battle with a keeper who had wielded a fork. The spieler, with an imitation diamond in his red tie, began:

"Ladies and Gentlemen! The first den contains the ferocious laughing hyenas and the largest brown

[10]

The Lion Tamer

bear in all the world. Denna Wyoming, the world-famous African lion tamer, will now enter their cage and put them through their unique performance."

I stood near the cage as Denna Wyoming came forward. I had never seen his face so stern. The breast of his blue velveteen coat was ornamented with many medals. He snapped a whip against his polished top boot. The band played.

He swayed slightly as he bowed. The crowd applauded. Wyoming's lip curled. It was the little hour of glory for which he lived—and worried. The laughing hyenas and brown bear were unimportant to him. It was his entrance into the lions' cage that bothered him. The lions were already pacing excitedly up and down their iron prison next door.

As the band played, Denna Wyoming slipped the bolt and entered the cage with the bear and hyenas. The brown bear lumbered from his corner. Suddenly Denna Wyoming slipped and fell. His arm hit the bear's snout. It lurched forward and grabbed him in a tenacious grip. The crowd, evidently thinking it was all part of the show, cheered loudly. The lions next-door roared. The snarling hyenas sprang at the recumbent figure of the lion tamer and bit viciously at his legs. The bear flung its body against the back of the cage. The lions stood on their hind-legs, their forelegs between the bars of their cage.

Soon everything was in confusion. Men yelled. Women fainted. Bob Cameron, the owner of the circus, hurried forward with a fork and prodded viciously at the animals. They paid no attention. The brown bear kept its grip, the hyenas snapped and tore. The white-washed wall became splotched with blood. I stood horrified.

Denna Wyoming moaned. The lions roared louder. The band played wails of discordant music.

The weazened ex-jockey dashed into the cage with a small board in his hand. His wrinkled and leather-tanned face was sterner than the lion tamer's had ever been. He stood erect and slashed the sharp board through the air. It tore a hyena's ear off. The hyenas both slouched away, jaws dripping. The brown bear let go its grip, and its head rolled from side to side as it backed away from its victim.

The lion tamer lay still. His velveteen coat was in shreds. His medals were dirty and disarranged. One boot had been torn from his leg. The ex-jockey dragged him to the door. Attendants placed him on a wooden shutter and hurried away. The lion

The Lion Tamer

tamer's heart quit pounding under his medals. The Big Guy had called his name.

The withered ex-jockey held the board aloft in his hand. The bear sat between the hyenas, who snarled in their corners.

"He'll be all right in a minute, folks—just a little accident."

He motioned to the band. It became silent.

"I'll now enter the cage with the forest-bred lions."

The band played louder. The ex-jockey went into the lions' cage with the small board in his hand. Having smelt blood, the lions puckered their noses.

"Work fast, you sons of Erin or I'll lop your ears off," snapped the ex-jockey.

His command cut the air like a knife. He hurried from the cage. "Bring me a drink—damn quick!" A flunky hurried for it.

When the crowd was disbanded he went to the dead lion tamer. Trailers had stolen the medals from his coat. He still clutched the little whip in his hand. Cameron, the circus owner, sent messengers ahead to a town in which we were to appear in three days. The death of the lion tamer would put money in his till.

The messengers announced that Denna Wyom-

Circus Parade

ing, the greatest lion tamer in the world, had been killed in mortal combat with six huge lions. His body would lie in state in the main tent in their fair city—a fit burial place for so brave a man. Lion tamers from Ringling's, Barnum's and John Robinson's circuses were hurrying to Texas to act as pallbearers at their great comrade's funeral. The town was placarded. The papers made headlines of the story.

We landed in the town with our dead lion tamer. He was laid out with one lone medal on his chest. It showed the Blessed Virgin holding the child Jesus. It was heavy and made of brass. Ten men were hired to play the part of the lion tamers from the other circuses. They were a frightful-looking crew. Two other lads and myself were made to act as their attendants. Bob Cameron seemed to have an idea that all lion tamers were Negroes. Nine of the pseudo-colleagues of the deceased were dark. The tenth was Irish. They paraded about the town like a minstrel troup. They drank an astonishing amount of liquor out of respect to their dead comrade. As I had respected him greatly, I drank also.

The circus grounds were jammed with people. They crowded into the main tent to see Denna Wyoming in his torn velveteen coat. The Homeric

[14]

The Lion Tamer

vagabond rose magnificently to the occasion. He sold verses in honor of his dead friend. They read:

Green lies the sod on Denna's breast,
And my poor heart is in a haze.
He sleeps in mansions of the blest,
Where lions in the meadows graze.

No more on earth will Denna play
His music to secure our praise.
But he will sing the years away
Where lions in the meadows graze.

As you are now—
So once was he,
As he is now—
So you will be.

It is our mighty
God's Great Plan—
Open thou thy heart—
Give what you can.

Thousands of people followed the coffin to a spot on a hill. A trained dog, drafted into service, watched, with tired eyes, the whips, spurs and boots

Circus Parade

of its supposedly dead master. A black preacher stood on a white tombstone and shouted:

"The Lawd Gawd he collect up the sons of Cain. He gatheh the little childern from play and from the dens of lions. When He say *Come*—you lays down youh work and go sailin' away to sit on the right hand of the Heavenly Fatheh and His Only Legitimate Son . . . glory be to Them each one!"

He stopped and scanned the motley assemblage with yellowish white eyes. "The Lawd giveth and the Lawd taketh away," he shouted. "That's fair enough," laughed a drunken stake driver, as the Negro minister of God continued with impressive manner, "May all heah see the light and the dark of their ways. . . . Fo' to them that hath shall be given some moah—and them that hain't got it never shall get it—world without end!—for so it is written—and ever will be—thus and ever—now and forever. He that lies here once held the lions in sway —and now none of you brethern is too pooh to do him honoh. . . ."

The lion tamer's body was lowered in the grave. The multitude poured back to the circus under the burning sun.

When the festivities ended the circus owner counted the receipts of the biggest day's business of

The Lion Tamer

the season. The crowd paid nearly two thousand dollars to see Denna Wyoming's funeral.

I sat on a flat car with the ex-jockey as the circus rattled out of the town. The wind flapped the canvas cover on a gilded wagon as he said, "Denna was a hell of a lion tamer . . . got killed by that damn brown bear!"

"I know . . . but how can you catch a blind bear's eye?" I asked.

His crooked mouth parted in a half-smile.

"I'm damned if I know," he replied.

II: Circus Parade

II: Circus Parade

CAMERON'S World's Greatest Combined Shows consisted of ten cars. The car which Cameron occupied had once been a Pullman. It was now obsolete. Cameron's bunk and office were in one end of the car. There were three state-rooms for important performers. Another room was occupied by Cameron's common-law wife. There were eight other sections in use. The open end of the car was used as a general dining and living room by day. At the other end was a small kitchen in which de Bussey, a French Negro, served as cook.

An old baggage car carried the ninety-foot "big top," the seventy-foot round top, and two thirty-foot middle pieces. It also carried stakes, poles, trunks, seats, lay-out pins and other paraphernalia. Flat cars carried the wagons in which stake-drivers and other circus roustabouts slept. The bunks were too full of vermin to be occupied long at a time, and so, weather permitting, they were not used.

The performers were more snobbish than any class of people I had ever known. They did not

[21]

Circus Parade

talk to the lesser gentry of the circus save only to give commands. They were known as "kinkers" to us. We looked upon them with mingled disdain and awe.

They "doubled in brass" in parade and band concert, each playing some musical instrument. For days at a time, when we were short of men, they also "doubled on canvas" or helped put up the tent.

Bob Cameron, the owner, was a remnant of early American circus days. He claimed to be seventy-three years old. His face was florid, his hair a faded brick red, his step firm and heavy. He was muscular and tall. His jaw was crooked, as though a blow had knocked it sideways.

His nose slanted in the opposite direction from his jaw. He was nearly blind in one eye. It had a streak across it; thin as a razor blade from one corner to the other. In vitality and gusto he was ageless. Sardonic and brutal, he cared for nothing on earth but his circus and the scarecrow woman who traveled with him as his wife.

She weighed about a hundred pounds, and was wrinkled, yellow and cracked like thin leather in the rain. Her face was not much larger than a sickly baby's. She looked to be ninety. Age had touched her with a wicked leer. One could have placed a

[22]

pencil in the hollow of her eyes, which were rheumy
and of a weird green color like a weed the frost had
touched. She had been a bare-back rider, and her
hands were overdeveloped. Her shoulders stooped
forward as she walked. Her nature, no larger than
herself, was mean and petty. The "Strong Woman"
had once called her a baby buzzard. It was the name
by which she was afterward known among us.

It was said that she had been married seven times.
She lived in her belligerent past. "I was born on
a horse's back—it's nobody's damn business when,"
she often said.

"The horse she was born on was sway-backed,"
was Jock's comment.

She helped to rule our vagabond world with a
ruthless snarl. Her special passion was to superintend the thieves in the gambling car. For long hours
at a time she would not leave the car which she occupied with Cameron. He gave her every attention.

Like Cameron, she seemed an undying type of humanity—all whalebone and gristle. Seventy years
on the road, the monotony of it often made her
mentally ill. Many times around the world, her
imagination was so limited that it was all of one
pattern to her. "It ain't no different—some people's
yellow and some's black and some's Irish," she used

to say. "It's all a heluva mess." She preceded every remark with a snarl.

In moods of mental illness she would lie and look out of the window with the defiant expression of an old hag that would not die. When some of my licentious doggerel had been shown to Cameron by the Lion Tamer, he decided that I would be a good companion for the Baby Buzzard, who loved everything in books that concerned illicit love. Her lascivious mind reeked with fantastic tales of sex. The only time her voice ever became soft was when she talked of some man out of the long ago.

"He knew how to love, you betcha,"—and then a deep sigh. "They were real men in them days." She would then lean her jaw on a withered arm and look defiantly at me as if anticipating that I would dispute her.

But my reply would always be, "You bet they were."

"Huh," would be the contemptuous rejoinder, followed by an expression that seemed to say, "What the hell do you know about it?"

Between helping Jock, the boss hostler, and now and then lending a hand in putting up or taking down the tent at the different towns, and my work as a crude secretary to the Baby Buzzard, besides running errands for the performers and freaks, I was kept busy.

The Baby Buzzard was not always easy to please. Seldom a day passed that she did not have an ache in some portion of her withered body. If I rubbed her back it seemed to cure the ache elsewhere. My wrists would become tired and numb. But the old lady would lie quite still under the rubbing and utter sounds which were neither moans nor purrs but blended of both. She was born for the wiles of an osteopath.

She would give me fifty cents after each rubbing. It was never in change, always the half-dollar. She was in the habit of keeping a dozen half-dollars about her always. They were placed in a glass, which she frequently picked up and rattled.

Once, as we were pulling into Houston, Texas, she lost the glass. The Baby Buzzard was in an agony of despair. Cameron sent for me. I had to rub her back for an hour. Cameron went away to help Silver Moon Dugan superintend the business of putting up the tent. My tired hands had finally rubbed the old lady to sleep. As I left the room, I stumbled upon an empty glass. Near it was a half-dollar. I picked up the money, and near it was another coin. I looked about patiently until I had found twelve of them. I placed them carefully in the glass and left the room taking glass and contents with me.

The old lady often mentioned "the damn thief that took my half-dollars" and wondered who he was.

I would always say, "Well you can't trust anything around a circus."

She would snarl and say, "Huh—what in hell do you know about it?"

Feeling that she was not the first woman to doubt the word of youth, I would say no more.

Cameron would always hold back the first four weeks salary. He would explain to all his employees that it was merely kindness on his part; that he did not wish anybody who worked for him to finish the season broke.

Seldom did the lesser workers have the fortitude to stick with the circus until the end of the season. If any of them endeavored to do so, they were "redlighted," thrown off the train near the red lights of a railroad yard. If they again managed to catch up with the show, they were promptly accused of desertion and run off the lot.

During the first four weeks Cameron would stand for an occasional "touch" on the part of his men.

Circus Parade

He would give them a quarter, a half-dollar, and once in a while a whole silver dollar at a time. In less than eight weeks the wandering circus laborers would learn that they were up against an unbeatable game in working for Bob Cameron, and would leave the show. As a result, all hands "doubled up."

Cameron paid the most honestly earned dollar reluctantly. It meant that much less money to be saved toward a larger show. He really did not dream of riches—only of a big circus.

His motto was: "As Big as Barnum's." Perhaps no more dishonest than many of the greater circus owners who had passed through the same school of trickery, Cameron had nevertheless been over forty years in acquiring a ten-car show.

It was said of him that he once came near to being in the big league of showmen but he cheated his partner, an illiterate Irishman, who believed in fairies, and was shrewder than a Jew.

An old circus roustabout told me that the Irishman, in retaliation, had made Cameron at the point of a gun, match a coin with him—best three out of five, for the entire circus. Cameron lost.

The Irishman's coin was the same on both sides.

Cameron discovered the trick. Twelve witnesses, all Irish, swore the game was fair. Cameron, mad with the slipping gold fever, tried to murder the Irishman.

The latter gentleman had playfully knocked his nose sideways, had cut his eye with a knife, and had then fractured his skull.

They were no longer friends. Cameron had to start all over again. The Irishman became honest and died rich.

It was said that after Cameron's split with his partner he succeeded in adding only one other car to his circus every four or five years. He still dreamed of a twenty-car show. And the years were crawling over him with mockery.

The approach of pay-day was like the hour of execution for Cameron. It mattered not whether business was good or bad—his greed mania was the same. His safe was guarded always by Slug Finnerty, Gorilla Haley, Silver Moon Dugan or some other circus ruffian even more dishonest, if possible, than himself.

Cameron sent all surplus cash to the bank in the town where he made his circus headquarters. He was a deacon in the Methodist church there, and a director in the bank.

Like many circus owners, he was respected in his winter headquarters' city. He brought business, money and wide advertising to the place.

He would hardly leave enough money to pay the men, if business lagged at all. And often he would allow the money to remain in the safe for several days after pay-day. Money was glue to Cameron.

Something had always happened to keep him from owning a "big show." A panic, the low price of cotton, ruined crops, cattle dying from drought. But once money was in the bank he drew it out with pain. He would hold a minimum in the bank. When down to that amount he would withdraw no more money if the heavens fell.

He could always wheedle the laborers. Somehow or other he could move the circus. But he could not give a show without the performers or "kinkers."

At one time Cameron had only left enough money in the safe to meet a pay-day that had passed. There was near mutiny in the circus, until Cameron announced two full weeks pay the next day.

The pay envelopes were ready in the next town. It was a small town in which no liquor was allowed to be sold. The next town in which we were to appear was wide open and wet.

Cameron knew the men would reach the wet town without breaking into their pay.

In the next town Bob Cameron borrowed a great

Circus Parade

deal of the money back from the men by offering them four weeks pay for two if business picked up.

Some of the men had a few dollars in their "grouch bags" which were made of chamois skin and tied about their necks. Circus rovers as a rule did not like people who saved money. They called them "grouchy." Hence the term "grouch bag."

And, of course, a grouch bag was a safe place in which to carry money. A circus is, or was, generally a canvas nest of petty thieves and criminals among the lower gentry.

Next to handing out money, Cameron deeply regretted giving passes to see his circus.

When he had a two-car and three-car show, he was always at war with railroad men. It was the same when he had a circus of ten cars. Train crews, like the rest of the world, enjoy sights that are free.

As he was stingy with passes to the crews who switched his train, often a switch engineer would wait until we were at breakfast and bump his engine into us. Cameron would shout his opinion of railroad men in general, but the mischief never abated. One train crew would pass the word on to the next division.

In earlier days Cameron often acted as his own

"advance man," and traveled ahead of his show. He was considered one of the best "fixers" in the business. A large circus will pay from five hundred to a thousand dollars a day to appear in a town. Some cities have been known to allow a circus to show free of charge in order to advertise the city.

Cameron's show would be called upon to pay from one to three hundred dollars tax, unless, of course, Cameron, or Bill Regan, his chief advance agent, managed to fix it for nothing. They would often be forced to give many passes away to city authorities. Regan always sent word back what the license fee would be, also the price of the "lot" rent, and other important information. If the advance man reports that a town is "tough," there is always the "fixer" in evidence.

Cameron was shrewd and resourceful in such matters. He always wore plaids or loud checked clothes. A gold watch chain, with links an inch long, was stretched across his vest. Two immense green elk teeth dangled from it. His hair was long and straggly. He wore a broad-brimmed Stetson hat. He was never without a heavy gold-headed cane. It was loaded with lead at the top. The cane had served as a weapon in many a circus battle.

Cameron's custom was to parade from the lot to

Circus Parade

the principal corner of the town in which he happened to be with his circus. After the band had played several selections, Cameron would mount a box and make a speech.

"Neighbors, it is sure a mighty good thing to be back once again in my old home state. Here in this my old state the sun kisses the meadows as with beams of silver. I was born over yonder about eighty miles. After all, neighbors and friends, I've toured all over the world and I want to tell you folks there ain't no state like the old state here after all. As I was saying to Senator ——, (mentioning a senator in Washington from the state in which he happened to be showing) God Almighty in his infinite wisdom made this state when he felt good. But, neighbors and friends, this state is the home of great showmen, and I want to tell you that never was there such a show on the road as you will see today. We have camels and tigers from Rotabasco, and lions from the Amazonian jungles of the Nile. We have the bloodsweating Behomoth also, The Strong Lady, gentle as a babe, and she can lift eleven men, such prodiverous strength was never before seen in the muscles of a lady. We also have the Moss Haired Girl, captured by me and my men on a hunting expedition in Absenteria."

[32]

Circus Parade

The band would play *Dixie* at the finish of the speech. The return to the circus lot was made over the leading street.

If the town had been lenient with the circus and had allowed a low license fee and cheap lot rent, Cameron would don his loud clothes after the parade and drop around to the saloons and hotel lobbies and become acquainted with as many people as possible. Always would he tell of his love for the state and of the present town in particular.

None of us ever learned just which corner of the world Cameron called home. He claimed as birth place every state in which his circus appeared.

But if the town was "tough" or had been none too generous, Cameron's system was not the same.

He would put on an old hat, a worn suit and run-down shoes. His diamonds and gold watch chain and other jewelry was left in the safe in the car in which he lived. The gold cane was also left behind. He would carry a gnarled hickory stick which resembled something recently cut from a tree. Thus prepared he would hasten to the mayor or the town clerk long before the parade was to start.

Cameron would take on a different appearance and actually look to be years older—a man drawn with illness. Once in the mayor's presence he would

Circus Parade

tell a sad tale of sickness and bad business and very gloomy prospects for the rest of the season. Nearly always he would leave with a license costing but a fraction of the regular price which other shows paid. And often the license was given for nothing.

If the mayor was too obdurate, Cameron's shoulders drooped more, his walk became more painful. He often limped. He would pace up and down in front of the town hall, or sit on the front steps, elbows on knees, head in hands. After attracting as much attention as possible, he would limp painfully before the local authorities. If the mayor or town clerk were present he would tell his story. If not, he would ask to have him sent to him, and explain that he was too ill to walk further. His tale was a masterpiece of pathos.

"I am old and ill and my days are about done. I am unable to pay salaries and if the license fee is large, my men will become charges in this my native state. I little dreamed that I as a boy would come to this. I wore the uniform of grey (or blue) for this state. It was at the battle of Shiloh that a bullet brought me the limp in my right leg." The authorities would look at his dejected appearance, and grant him that which he wished.

The result was generally a free license. No mayor

Circus Parade

wanted a show stranded in his town. The mayor would often send for the owner of the lot upon which the show was playing. The rent would be made cheaper. Sometimes the grocer and the butcher reduced their prices also.

If the mayor was "too Scotch or churchy" or "a Christer," as Cameron would say—the circus owner would wear the makeup all day. Usually, however, when the license was given and the rent reduced, Cameron would return to the car and don his loudest checked raiment. In one town, after Cameron had changed clothes and was talking in front of the main tent, the mayor approached and asked him solicitously about the old man who had appeared at the city hall. Cameron never forgot the compliment.

Once Cameron failed dismally in all efforts to get a cheaper license or not. Neither was he to be allowed to parade until the license money was paid. In this case it was three hundred dollars. "God Almighty," yelled Cameron, "I wouldn't pay three hundred dollars for Bill Bryan as a freak." The rent for the lot was also exorbitant.

Cameron learned that the county line was close to the town.

He soon discovered that there was no county license for tent shows. In less than an hour he had

Circus Parade

arranged for a lot and the show played both per-formances.

Though Cameron pleaded, the town, governed by religious fanatics, would not allow the "sinful circus" to parade.

The lot which Cameron secured was a mile from the railroad yards where we unloaded. We were told to get ready as if for parade and start for the cir-cus grounds at eleven that morning.

We made our way slowly down the main street, the band playing, the circus wagons rumbling.

The chief of police rode up on a large white horse.

"What do you mean by paradin' when we told you not to?" he yelled.

"We're not paradin'," replied Cameron blandly, "we are within the law in going to a lot which we have rented honorably and without malice afore-thought."

"You're all arrested," screamed the chief. "I'll show you that you can't make fun of the laws of ―――."

"I don't wanta be unkind, brother, but don't you see it'll break the town feedin' this bunch?" said the suave Cameron while the circus parade stretched several blocks away awaiting entrance to the city jail. The chief hastily held a parley with other of-

[36]

Circus Parade

ficials. Cameron's circus was allowed to turn about
and make its way to the circus grounds while the
band played the battle cry of the circus, to the blare
of clarinet and fife and roar of drum:

'Twas just about ten years ago,
Too early yet for ice or snow;
Thru' bounteous Texas coming down,
A circus with a funny clown.
          "Hey Rube"

The boys warn't feeling very well,
The reason why I cannot tell,
And as they made each little town,
They whispered when the "Gawks" came round
          "Hey Rube"

It's a little phrase, 'tis true;
Its meaning well each faker knew
And e'en the weakest heart was stirred,
At mention of that magic word,
          "Hey Rube"

"They'll eat you up in this 'ere town,
The boys'll tear your circus down,"

Circus Parade

Thus spoke a man with hoary head.
The main "Guy" winked, and softly said
"Hey Rube"

They gathered round, about three score,
I am not sure but there were more,
Red-hot and eager for the fray;
The boys all thought, but didn't say
"Hey Rube"

The ball was opened, like a flash,
Above the battle's din and dash,
As a thunderbolt hurled from the sky,
Rang loud and long the battle cry,
"Hey Rube"

'Twas finished; the smoke rolled away,
As clouds before the sun's bright ray;
That Texan chivalry was gone
They couldn't sing that circus song,
"Hey Rube"

"Gawks, Guys, and Rubes," another day
When e'er a circus comes your way,
And you are "spillin' " for a "clem,"
Be sure they haven't learned to sing,
"Hey Rube"

Circus Parade

It was the battle cry of the circus. And no war song ever called more ruthless barbarians to slaughter. Events in circus life were often dated from great "Hey Rube" encounters. All citizens were called rubes by circus people.

III: Hey Rube!

III: Hey Rube!

THERE were some people with Cameron's Circus whom the corrosion of years could not rob of fine qualities. But the greater number were thieves, liars and embryo yeggs. Desperadoes known as "cannons," "dips" and "guns" followed us to every town.

Women, faded, beautiful and wanton, lovers of their own kind, and men-loving men, all trekked with Cameron's, living generally with the ethics and filth of gypsies.

Each and all of us, shrewd or stolid, traded upon the imbecilities of human nature and had comtempt for it as a result. Honor, to us, was a word in a dictionary.

A group of whining morons with the cunning of foxes were ever at our heels. They were known as "Monday men." As the family washing was generally done on Monday, they would steal it from the line and sell it to those it might almost fit.

All about was the odor of long unbathed bodies;

Circus Parade

and clothing stiff from perspiration that had turned white like salt.

We had struck a "rainy season"—the nightmare of circus life. With insufficient heat in dripping weather, the same clothing became soaking wet and dried on our bodies. We forestalled pneumonia with rot gut whisky and lungs that pumped hard with a zest for life. For the most part we clung like animals to that which we accepted without a thought.

The high class gamblers and crooks were known as the "Bob Cameron men." They consisted of the ticket sellers, card sharks and dice experts. They gave ten per cent. of their earnings to Cameron. He mistrusted and hated all of them. But as he paid them no salary, and they were a source of revenue, he had a thief's toleration for his kind. They lived in a car of their own.

The "Square Johns" were the canvas men and other laborers. They were given the name with complimentary contempt because they worked hard. The vast majority of them were potential crooks whom labor and stolidity had made submissive.

The spielers worked in league with the "dips" or pickpockets.

Whenever a large group of rustics would assemble the spieler would say, "Now, Ladies and Gentle-

Hey Rube!

men, we aim to run an honest show—but as you perhaps know there are thieves in high and low places—and dishonest people may follow us—just as you may have dishonest people right here in your own fair city. Hence and therefore—I warn you to watch out for your pocketbooks and other valuables."

Immediately rustic hands would feel for purses. The pickpockets would watch where the hands went, and follow after.

Slug Finnerty was the chief spieler. He had lost an eye in a brawl many years before. The empty socket was red and criss-crossed with scars. He was deeply pock-marked and stoop-shouldered. His ears had been pounded until they resembled pieces of putty clinging to his bald and cone-shaped head. An ex-bruiser of the old school, he had served five years in a southern penitentiary for a crime unspeakable. The boy was injured internally.

Slug was the money-lender and the leader of the gang of crooks. The Baby Buzzard despised him. She was the one person with courage enough to greet him with a snarl. He had once called her a "damned old bag of bones" in the presence of Cameron. The owner of the show turned white, then red, then walked away.

Circus Parade

After this incident it was always said that Slug knew where Cameron "had buried the body." Our meaning implied that Slug knew of a murder or other crime that Cameron had committed in some part of the world, and that Cameron was afraid he would tell.

At any rate, Slug had been with the show for many seasons. He was said to be the greatest short-change artist in the canvas world. He robbed every citizen who did not produce the exact price for a ticket. When making change he had a habit of turning his empty socket toward the victim. It was a ghastly sight. It had the proper psychological effect upon his victim.

He had a trick of folding a bill in his hand. He would count both ends in the presence of a patron. In this manner a ten dollar bill was made into twenty dollars. Another unerring method was the "two-bit short change." He would return change of a five dollar bill by counting "one-two-three-four" swiftly. By the time he had counted out three dollars he would say—"and four"—there you are." The customer having heard the word "four" so often would conclude that Slug meant four dollars and pocket the change—short one dollar. Always near Slug was the "rusher"—a man who kept the patrons moving swiftly, once they had been given their change.

Slug was an adept pocket-picker. He could slug and "roll" or rob a drunkard in record time. Hence his nickname. It was all he was ever known by. He was also a past master at the manipulation of loaded dice, marked cards or the shell game. His earnings at the end of each season were on a par with Cameron's. He was always ready to loan money at fifty per cent. interest. Cameron would always turn the employee's money over to Slug. They divided the interest and all other profits. The two men hated each other.

Most of the borrowers of Slug's money spent it for liquor or cocaine. As long as they owed Cameron or Finnerty money they were not "red-lighted."

Slug was a furtive bootlegger in the dry sections. He would give the alcoholics a few drinks, and once their appetites were aroused he would then sell them more and loan them money with which to buy it.

Rosebud Bates was always in the clutches of the one-eyed Shylock. His mania for musical contraptions kept him penniless. He had joined the show in a small Colorado town in the early spring. He was a trap drummer. Decidedly effeminate, with a

Circus Parade

pink and white complexion, the strict moral gentlemen with the show at once became suspicious of
Rosebud. With no evidence upon which to base the
charge, they immediately called him a "fairy." The
accusation stuck. Our world was brutal, immoral,
smug and conventional. We had unbounded
contempt for all those who did not sin as we
sinned.

Rosebud's parents had spent a great deal of
money on his musical education. He could play
many musical instruments. His passion in the end
became a trap drum. Finnerty called him Master
Bates. At each greeting he would say, "How are
you, Master Bates?" amid laughter. Bates would
blush and remain quiet.

Rosebud would spend hours in imitating the
whistle of a locomotive, the song of a bird, the
roar of a lion, with different musical contraptions.

He was always surrounded with noise-producing
instruments. One extravagance had cost him three
hundred dollars. They were a set of tympanies or
"kettle drums." He had seen the instruments in a
store in Dallas. So great was his passion that he
borrowed the money of Slug at fifty per cent. interest.

Rosebud could juggle his drum sticks as he

drummed. This was one of the features of the parade which Cameron quickly recognized.

Those who called Rosebud effeminate were correct in their judgment of him.

It was in an Oklahoma town. Our canvas roof quivered under the heat of the sun. He told me of his ailment.

"You won't tell no one, will you?" he pleaded.

"No—I'll not say a word," was my reply.

He looked doubtfully at me. "You know they'd run me off the lot if they knew."

"I know—and they're not a damn bit better themselves—look at Finnerty—he'd be the first to slug you. But Jock would understand—you could talk to him. He's been through hell and back agin."

"But I won't talk to him now," was Rosebud's hesitating answer. "I'll just buy a lot more instruments and forget." He polished a drum stick. "Playin' a trap drum's better than blowin' your heart out on a wind like the clarinet, anyhow. Those poor devils in the band have to play when their mouths are all sore. I've seen 'em blow fever blisters right through the instruments—and all for fifteen dollars a week," he grunted.

It was our second day in the city. Life was easier when the circus played three days in a town. Release

Circus Parade

from pitching the tent and traveling gave us a chance to rest. We looked ahead for many weeks to such three-day periods of rest.

"What causes it, Rosebud?" I asked, coming back to the one question.

He looked plaintive, with drawn face.

"I don't know," he answered slowly, "I've heard a lot of reasons. I never did like girls as far back as I can remember. Then when I got older it got worse. I used to like to nurse when I was five years old. It got so it was my mother's way of rewarding me for being good. It never failed with her. I didn't get any nourishment—just the sensation. Mother never understood. I didn't either—then. And now of course I can't tell her. She teaches Sunday School and belongs to a club in Denver."

I became Rosebud's friend and talked to Jock about him.

"Please don't say a word to anyone," I begged of Jock.

"Not me, Kid. I won't say a word. It's Rosie's own business."

Jock's words and attitude toward Rosebud gave me more sympathy for Rosebud and helped strengthen my early tolerance for the vagaries of sex.

[50]

Hey Rube!

The Baby Buzzard was kind to Rosebud. Whether this sprang from a sense of hatred toward Finnerty or a generous impulse I could not tell.

The third day came in a drizzle of rain. Finnerty was in a sullen mood. The audience was small, which gave him less chance to short-change the patrons.

A surly oil worker claimed that Slug had short-changed him. Slug was indignant at the charge. With persuasive tongue he apparently proved to the man that he was wrong.

After the man had gone Rosebud appeared with his drum before a small tent a short distance from where Finnerty was taking tickets. The rain had made the drum heads damp. His sticks lacked the usual bounce and slipped out of his hands several times as he tried to juggle them. Finnerty leered across at him—"Master Bates! Cut out that damned noise."

Rosebud disappeared at once, murmuring to me, "Some day I'll break a drum over his head."

The rain still drizzled before the evening show.

The oil worker who had been short-changed in the afternoon now stood near Finnerty's ticket wagon with a half-dozen other men.

Finnerty shouted with pleading voice: "Step

Circus Parade

right up, Ladies an' Gentlemen! Here's your tickets —the show is about to start."

The clouds hung low and black. The rain drizzled faster. Seven other men joined the group which watched Finnerty. The short-change artist acted as unconcerned as possible. A voice louder than the rest exclaimed:

"We'll tear down the God damn tent!"

I looked in the direction of the voice. It was that of the man who had been robbed by Finnerty of less than a dollar.

A feeling of impending trouble came over me. Rosebud joined me.

"There's over a dozen big guys out in front," I said to Rosebud. "It looks like they're goin' to rush Finnerty."

Suddenly there was a crash. The oil workers charged Finnerty in a body.

Finnerty just had time to shout the menacing "Hey Rube!" Instantly the circus grounds were furiously alive. To distinguish themselves from the "rubes," a few members of the circus began tying white handkerchiefs around their necks. The code was—not to strike a man with a handkerchief about his neck. The method failed to work in this fight. The men became too vicious.

Hey Rube!

Men ran in every direction. It was like the beating of tom-toms in African hill country. No longer were the circus employees prowling members of organized society. They had forgotten that Bob Cameron cheated them. Facing the common enemy every man from Cameron down picked up a "staub" or tent stake, the upper end of which was encircled with an iron band.

More than a dozen other men joined the "rubes."

"Cut the ropes an' drop the tent," a "rube" yelled. The rubes thought the ropes alone held the tent. They were mistaken.

They ran with knives and slashed at the canvas sides. They cut the ropes which were tied to the stakes. Women and children screamed and fainted. Some crawled under the side-walls of the tent. The clouds lowered. The wind shifted to the west and rose in velocity. A streak of lightning jagged down the sky. A roar of thunder followed.

Finnerty's blue ticket wagon was kicked to pieces.

Two men grabbed the money drawer and yelled, "We'll teach 'em to rob our buddy—we will."

Others screamed as they ran around the main tent with knives. Soon the side walls had been slashed to ribbons. The leader of the mob, a heavy and agile man, yelled above the roar of wind and

[53]

Circus Parade

rain, "Rush in there fellows an' cut the main guy ropes—we'll slump her in the middle—we'll teach these crooks to rob us."

Cameron and Finnerty stood near where the cash drawer had been. They fought valiantly in the midst of enemy and friend.

Benches were upturned in the main tent, the center pole toppled, and soon the vast canvas crumpled like a wet rag, the wind whistling around it.

Boards, maul handles, quarter poles, every instrument imaginable was used in the frightful welter.

Rosebud had not taken time to put his drum away. A club crashed through it and made an explosion as of thunder. Rosebud heard the noise and fell wailing over the broken drum. A man grabbed him by the collar and yanked him upward.

"You God damn murderer," Rosebud screamed as he turned around and jumped toward the man. Both his hands stretched outward like the paws of an angry cat. His fingers became stiff as his nails dug bloody gashes in his antagonist's face. The man fought furiously and soon Rosebud fell backward, his head hitting the hard sides of his drum. He sighed deeply and lay still.

The man turned from Rosebud to join his com-

Hey Rube!

rades in a combined attack on Finnerty and Cameron. With a catlike spring he grabbed Finnerty around the throat. Together they rolled to the ground, heavy fists thudding. Finnerty, a blood-streaked madman now, threw his right fist upward. It crashed against his attacker's chin and he crumpled near Rosebud's body.

Finnerty stood like an immense one-eyed gorilla about to spring and snarled between oaths, "Come on you, God damn rubes, and meet your master!"

A man circled behind him with a club. It went upward and downward while Finnerty dodged. The momentum of the intended blow threw the man off his feet for a second. Before he gained his poise Finnerty walked in close, his teeth grinding, his tongue licking the blood from his battered upper lip. His two fists struck with horrible precision on each side of the man's jaws. The head went backward as if pulled suddenly with a rope. As he fell unconscious Finnerty kicked him twice in the groin. Still enraged, Finnerty then pounced upon him and drove his fist straight downward. The blow covered the man's entire face with blood.

"Look out, Slug," a voice yelled, and now the bloody monster turned swift as a tiger. Two men engaged him in battle. Their fists crashed against his face. He fought them both viciously without moving backward. The band stand toppled over.

The two men had placed the money drawer in the stand while they returned to the fight.

The coins scattered everywhere. Many, more eager for gold than battle, scampered after it. Cameron had fought near the stand until it fell. Then, seeing money scattered on the ground he rushed madly at those who tried to pick it up. Jock had by this time come upon the scene. He charged into the fight. Seeing Rosebud unconscious, he carried him out of the fracas.

Someone, whether stake-driver or Rube, had crashed a club against Cameron's head. He waved from side to side, but stood up under the thudding impact. Another blow caught him across the back. A man of seventy-three, heavily ruptured and wearing a truss, he sank downward and remained on his knees by a tremendous effort of will. Then, too weak to remain in that position, he rolled over on his back and made an effort to pull his truss and the heavy weight upon it into place. Rising, he clutched at his groin with one hand, and swung a "staub" with the other. At last, fully conscious, but unable to move, Cameron lay still and blasphemed. His oaths could be heard above the noise of the conflict.

[56]

Hey Rube!

"Come on, boys," he yelled, "we can't let the God damn ratty rubes lick us." A man kicked at his face. He rolled over, groaning with pain, and protected it with his arms.

Jock rushed up yelling to the man, "Come an' battle a man that's on his feet." The heavier man rushed Jock but fell writhing from the effects of two blows delivered far below his waist line.

The general noise and confusion attracted the women. The Strong Woman rushed at the enemy who retreated before her. She moved about, an infuriated four-hundred-pound giantess, her hair streaming, wet and bedraggled in the rainy night.

Finnerty, now battered beyond recognition, fought on, though too weak to take command. It fell to Jock who was soon joined by the Baby Buzzard.

"Hello Betsy," shouted Cameron upon beholding her as she slashed at the enemy with a long blacksnake whip.

"Tell Goosey to bring the elephants," Cameron yelled.

Soon two elephants charged across the lot, each holding the end of a thirty-foot pole.

Cameron lay in the path of one of the elephants.

Circus Parade

The Baby Buzzard tried to drag him away. Cameron crawled out of danger on his knees.

Goosey rushed the elephants through the crowd while friend and foe scampered before them. They retreated with curses and moans.

The enemy rushed off the lot pursued by Goosey and his two elephants and a roaring crowd of circus roustabouts.

They barricaded themselves in a small rickety barn. It was soon completely demolished and its occupants beaten until they were unconscious.

Silver Moon Dugan, the boss canvasman, gathered his fighting forces and entrained the circus.

An engineer hauled it to a place of safety on a far siding.

Lights were dimmed and the train guarded until the chief despatcher gave us an engine and the right of way.

Cameron's loss was several thousand dollars. Finnerty had gained eighty cents.

IV: The Moss-Haired Girl

IV: The Moss-Haired Girl

WE reached ——, Missouri, in a worn condition. The news of our battle had preceded us in the newspapers. Cameron was unable to leave his bed. Finnerty's one eye was completely closed. He could not see for several days. But his spirit was indomitable. He was the first to appear on the new lot.

We dispensed with the parade until mid-afternoon and spent the morning mending the main tent. After buying all the half-inch rope that could be had in the town, we again painted the tents with paraffine to make them waterproof. The canvas was two seasons old and had begun to leak.

When all was nearly ready for the parade, a deputation of citizens arrived and asked for the proprietor. Upon being shown to his car they informed him that he was forbidden to show in the town. We were billed in the place for two days. Cameron used all his eloquence and tricks on the men. They remained firm. Telegrams from the Oklahoma city gave reports of our hey rube fight with biased detail.

[61]

Circus Parade

The performers and other aristocrats with the show were indignant at such treatment by the rubes. But we who had the hard work to do were glad. Our next jump was one of four hundred miles on a third-class railroad. The trip would consume the better part of two days and nights. It would give us a respite in the incessant round of toil and turmoil.

But Cameron found work for idle hands to do.

We spent the first day mending the tents and seats and in rubbing pained black and blue spots on our bodies with arnica and liniment.

There was a gash in Rosebud's body which had been inflicted when he fell on the edge of his drum. He sat with a heavy bandage around it, while he polished his drum sticks and cleaned his other musical contraptions. Late in the afternoon he walked wearily into the town with his broken drum.

With Jock's consent I divided my time between Cameron, Finnerty, the Strong Woman and the Moss-Haired Girl. The latter had been struck by a flying club which had fractured her rib.

As she shared with the Strong Woman the honors of being Cameron's most valuable freak, she was treated with consideration.

The Moss-Haired Girl

"Why don't you sue the broken-nosed old devil?" Buddy Conroy, who operated the loaded dice game under Finnerty, had asked her.

"No, no, I wouldn't do that. The old faker has troubles enough. Besides, I'm of age. I should have kept out of the way of the club. Anyhow, he was blind when he threw it."

"Maybe Finnerty threw it because he couldn't never make a date with you."

"No, he was just blind, that's all," was Alice's rejoinder.

I worked about the tent until Conroy left.

Then the Moss-Haired Girl turned to me, saying:

"Heavens, I'm glad he's gone. He gives me a cold feeling—like a dead fish."

"Yeap," I said, "he's as bad as Finnerty."

The girl laughed. "No, he's not that bad. There's nothing as bad as Finnerty—but then—maybe we don't understand."

Few people knew the Moss-Haired Girl's real name. To the circus people she was known as Alice Devine. Her mother had been Swedish, her father Indian and Irish. She was the most superior person with the circus, and the weirdest. She converted her hair, which was between blonde and brown, and

[63]

long, into a tangled heap of moss by washing it frequently in stale beer, which she tinted green with herbs.

Cameron gave her seventy-five dollars a week and all expenses, and billed her as "The Moss-Haired Girl." The women flocked to see her in every town. She also earned about fifty dollars a week by selling portraits of herself.

Her eyes were a deep blue, her complexion dark, her body graceful, her face beautiful.

She read a great deal, and often loaned books to the Strong Woman and the Baby Buzzard.

The Moss-Haired Girl talked to me often. Her life was as empty as an unused grave. But, with many opportunities, she seemed to desire no change. She did her washing twice a week. She always left silk underclothing and dresses to be cleaned and expressed to her in the next town. She would arrange each week about the buying of beer, which she allowed to grow stale. She bought many different magazines.

Looking back on her now I realize that she was repressed but deeply emotional. She loved all that pertained to life and hated philosophy. "It's all rot," she used to say. "None of them know a bit more about things than I do."

The Moss-Haired Girl

Now that the fogs of twenty years have cleared away, I see much that I have lost and little that I have gained. Then, I was but a day or two from hunger and destitution. Now they are years away. But something else has happened. The brain has grown tired. The ennui of life is everywhere. Adventure lurked around every corner then, and life was wild and free. I often went to my canvas bunk with muscles that ached and legs that dragged wearily. But each morning opened on a new world—and many tales were told.

The Moss-Haired Girl, the Strong Woman, Aimee, the Beautiful Fat Girl, The Lion Tamer, Whiteface, Lefita and Jock are people that I shall never meet again. But I would trade the empty honor of a writer's name to be once again their comrade.

There was something in the girl which I was not mature enough to fully appreciate at the time. Her eyes squinted often, as the eyes of people will who have spent early years in a desert country. She had reverted to the lethargy of the Indian and loved to live in a tent. Her cleanliness of body must have been derived from her Swedish mother.

The Moss-Haired Girl had been born in a little desert town of Arizona. Her father was a railroad

[65]

Circus Parade

engineer who fell in love with a brakeman's wife and ran away. He was never heard of again. Alice was five years of age at this time. Her mother struggled through and managed to live by running a small restaurant.

When Alice was seven her mother became converted to Catholicism, and within a year the small daughter began her life at a convent.

An old nun, part Indian, became fond of her. The little girl fell in with the routine of the convent, and with stoical silence absorbed everything. The aged nun was in charge of the linen department, and Alice spent hours with her in the sewing room. It was her duty to thread the needles for her old friend, whose eyes were watery and weak.

The nun's black habit hid her sparse grey hair and projected two inches out from her forehead. Her mentality was hardly above a child's. She owned five rosaries and spent much time in shining the naked brass bodies of Christ which hung upon them.

Always she talked of Christ as though he had been an Indian. She called him the Great Firebuilder. Some day he would come and burn to cinders all the Irish in the world. For they were the people who in her opinion had crucified Christ.

[66]

The Moss-Haired Girl

There were several old Irish nuns in the convent who gossiped a great deal. Sister Marie did not like them.

Often, when the little girl had threaded the needle, the decrepit black-hooded woman would hold it aloft and talk of the Great Firebuilder.

"He come down—way down—and stay on top o' San Francisco mountain—he throw a torch and burn all up but you an' me an' Indian people like us . . . he give us back America an' all the fish in the sea—an' never no more houses and things, but like birds we be free. An' Gabriel' come back o' Jesu' and blow big horn an' all people go right in fire an' they'll all go. 'Oh blesse' Jesu' she burn an' burn—an' the big voice roll down the moumtan an' scare the eagles an' it'll say, 'This is but water compare to the everlastin' fire. A million times hotter it be—so hot—the desert is cool in July'—Then the fire will go out an' big green trees and water in brooks and little white birds will be all aroun'. Then camps'll be an our people livin' in them."

Then in a moment of exaltation she would clasp the little girl in her arms and squeeze her so tightly that Alice felt like screaming.

Alice often cried in the night when she thought of the Irish people being burned up. She thought,

Circus Parade

of course, that there were only two classes of people in the world, the Irish and the Indians.

Once the old nun gave her a huge and beautiful wax doll. She slept with it five months and smoothed its blonde hair and washed its immense blue eyes every morning and evening. She called it Lullaba-lie.

One Friday she was called quickly for noon-day devotion and left the doll sitting with perfect poise at the end of the arbor. In fifteen minutes, as Alice prayed, the sun crawled around the arbor, and the wax doll melted like the Irish in the Great Fire-builder's flame.

Alice ran away from the chapel in the direction of her doll. Two little marble-blue eyes and a yellow wig were all that was left. The child stood for a moment, then clasped its hands, started to cry, held the tears back and sank down near the heap of wax. The sun burned her bare arms, but she sat for a long time, as still as a beautiful little female Buddha.

Something drove something out of the little girl's soul at this moment. What it was I do not know, and neither could she ever explain. She was an Indian and a Swede, and to explain it one would be forced

[68]

The Moss-Haired Girl

to explore long damned-up and century-old rivers of emotion. Her finely chiseled little mouth went tighter. She rose, and absentmindedly tried to pull a skirt over her knees. She wore bloomers at the time, but she obeyed a habit imbedded in her by long dead female ancestors.

She picked up the little blonde wig and dropped it. She then picked up the little blue eyes. They rattled in her hand. She kissed them all over, then placed them in her waist pocket over her heart.

She walked slowly under the blazing Arizona sun toward the sewing-room. The old nun was polishing the largest figure of Christ she owned. The little girl staggered half blindly toward her and held out the two marble blue eyes.

Not a word was said for a long time. Then the old lady held the little girl's face in her wrinkled hands in such a manner that all that could be seen of it were the red lips and the small pearl upper teeth. She leaned down and put her leathery mouth against the girl's and sobbed:

"O Jesu', Jesu', Jesu'—you take Lullaba-lie all home."

Alice said no word. She put the marble eyes back in her pocket. That night she placed them in a little

Circus Parade

pine box, wrapped about with cotton. Each morning she would open the box and look at them. She carried the marble eyes for eighteen years.

When she was twelve years old Alice knew nothing of her body. When nature worked a change in it she was dreadfully frightened. She washed her clothes in cold water and put them on again hurriedly. Pneumonia developed and for three weeks Sister Marie nursed her day and night. She passed the crisis in the fourth week and slowly recovered.

Out of her head six days, she heard Irish bodies sizzling in a fire built by a red-headed man thousands of feet high. She saw him blow clouds away from his eyes that he might see.

The convent would sail through the air for hours at a time.

Sister Marie had changed into the most beautiful of young angel women. She flew constantly about Alice's head.

Sister Marie broke down when Alice became convalescent. When Alice became strong again, the old nun died.

Alice heard the news. Her lithe young body went rigid and fell.

In three days Sister Marie had five rosaries wrapped about her worn and scrawny hands. She

The Moss-Haired Girl

was placed before the cheap gilt altar in the chapel.

A nun stood on each side of Alice as she looked at the body of her friend. There was a faint smile on the old nun's lips, as though she saw the Irish burning. The gossipy old nuns were now tearful.

The priest told of God's work, while sun shadows danced across the chapel and burned the lamp of the sanctuary a rubier red.

The pensive girl listened, and as the priest talked her mood turned into one of whimsical sadness. Above her red and blue angels flew around the mighty figure of God seated in a chair which was enveloped in a white cloud. Sister Marie was with him, and after all she was happier. And Alice half wished she also were up with God.

The high chapel ceiling, painted by a rustic artist to represent God ruling the starry heavens, was a never-failing source of wonder to Alice.

Sister Marie had told her about the man who had painted the ceiling. "He had a long white beard an' he talked like a German an' he worked up there weeks an' weeks an' weeks an' once they came in the chapel an' he was kneelin' down in front of the great figure of God—us sisters all thought God's face looked sadder in the picture after that. . . ."

The priest's voice brought Alice from revery. The

Circus Parade

priest, a powerful man, held his arm high. Silver and green embroidery glistened under his white surplice. That hour was burned forever in the memory of Alice. The priest remained a symbol of all manhood to her. She confused him with God—and held ever afterward the blending of the two as her great unknown lover.

At twenty-seven, in spite of vicious environments, save for rough repartee now and then, she was still clean of heart and mind—as virginal as Sister Marie. The old nun had often talked of being "married to God." Years later the Moss-Haired Girl said, "He's really the Great Lover—no worry of children or sickness—and never any desertion—and always *understanding*—and if you lose in the end —and He's only an illusion—you've had the fun of kidding yourself a whole lifetime—that in itself is *God!*"

The sermon ended, the priest threw holy water over the long sleeping Sister Marie.

The body was borne out of the chapel, the convent girls following, and then the nuns, and then the priest and his altar boys. The palms of all hands were pressed tightly together, the fingers pointing upward, while the priest's heavy voice could be

The Moss-Haired Girl

heard above the musical girlish voices of Alice and her comrades in the beautiful Te Deum.

Sister Marie was placed in a square black hearse while her friends followed in dilapidated busses which rumbled over the yellow sand to a slight elevation dotted with palms, sagebrush and cactus. Far away the tops of mountains glimmered radiant white in the sun.

It was early spring on the desert. The immense yellow valley seemed a shining mirror upon which was painted green, yellow, red, and gold patches of wildflowers, soon to fade like Alice's doll under the sun's torrid flame. The vastness, the immensity, crept into Alice, which, combined with her repressed grief, made her silent for days—and gave her, for the rest of her life, a touch of greatness and understanding.

The priest looked about when the desert sand had finished rattling on Sister Marie's coffin. Alice rushed up to him, breaking the stillness of the desert with a wail. "Father, father—she's gone—oh, oh—she's gone . . ." She sobbed violently, her cheek against his surplice.

The kindly and good man brushed the grey hair out of his eyes, as Alice, still sobbing convulsively, her beautiful young body shaking, now knelt before him.

Wind and sun-tanned nuns and girls budding into full life gathered about the two.

"It's all right, Alice dear," the gentleman said, "lean on me as you would on your Heavenly Father. She is not gone—all the rolling seas cannot wash her memory away—she is no more gone, Alice dear, than you are gone—that which God has made to live and breathe can never disappear. You see, dear child, we are merely serving Him here for a little while—then we too shall go away to take up our work elsewhere—with more love for beauty and service—on and on and on—eternally serving in our Master's cause." He placed his hand on Alice's head. She rose with wet eyes and clung to him.

All silently returned to the convent.

Looking back in the direction of the cemetery Alice saw a great ship sailing high in the desert air above Sister Marie's grave. A beautiful city and a golden port stretched miles to the west. Another and another ship joined the first. In each vessel were beautiful angels with faces pink and white, clear cut as cameos, and garlanded with flowers. And as she looked, another city formed in the sky. The

[74]

streets were an indigo blue, and all the people, plainly seen, were more beautiful than the finest illustrations in her fairy books.

Immense trees grew everywhere and on their branches hung roses of every shape and color. Birds larger than condors, brilliant and many colored, flew lazily and majestically above the golden-green and blue cities.

And as Alice gazed, the birds formed in squadrons and darted downward to Sister Marie's grave. It opened wide and there emerged a beautiful Indian girl a few years older than Alice. It looked to the girl like Sister Marie must have looked in the long ago.

Her limbs and body were as shapely as the statue of Saint Teresa in Father Maloney's study. Her eyes were as radiant as the sun and her hair, a bluish black, rippled as though fanned by the wings of larks.

The girls waited until the young Sister Marie raised her arms. She was lifted suddenly and gracefully into the air and rested on the back of the most beautiful bird of all. Each bird stretched out its wings and made no other motion. Sister Marie, on the large bird in the centre, sat upright and waved her hands at Alice as all the birds, wings out-

Circus Parade

stretched and motionless, sailed swifter than light above the streets of the golden cities.

"Father, Father," exclaimed Alice, "I see Sister Marie! . . . she is very beautiful."

The priest caressed the girl. "That is her soul, dear child, going back to God." Then slowly, "The soul of Sister Marie was always beautiful."

Alice no longer loved the convent.

Sister Marie had always been fond of Alice's hair. She tried every method she could contrive to make it more beautiful. It reached to her knees.

At an amateur theatrical after Lent, in the convent, Alice appeared as the Moss-Haired Girl. The aged nun knew the nature of many herbs and wildflowers. By a process of her own, she had combined some concoction with two bottles of stale beer which the priest had discarded, and washing Alice's hair with the solution, it was made to resemble moss. The other girls were mystified. Sister Marie gave the secrets of her formula to Alice who had occasion afterwards to use it often.

Alice always enjoyed seeing beautiful hair. Once, in the convent, after a young woman had taken her final vows, Alice climbed on a ladder and saw two nuns cutting away long strands of sunny blonde hair. Alice felt sad for days.

The Moss-Haired Girl

Two years later Father Maloney's soul was borne away by the birds.

Alice left the convent and grew tired of her harsh mother in two months. More and more as she grew older did she revert to the ways of the Indian. With a good singing voice, she joined a carnival company. Life in a tent appealed strongly to her. Once, when too hoarse to sing, she washed her hair with the solution and became the leading attraction with the carnival.

And thus was born the beautiful Moss-Haired Girl, who delighted thousands of women twice ten years ago.

V: Murder for Pity

V: Murder for Pity

W E left ——, and traveled leisurely to ——.
Our train literally crawled through the
Ozark region of Missouri. Cameron stormed at the
slow pace and feared we would arrive a day late.

"Let the old devil worry," said Jock. "Maybe
some other guy'll get killed an' he can cash in
again."

There were seven of us in the open door of a
horse car. It was a happy time in our lives—an
oasis that made our vagabond hearts pump fast.
There would be no care and little work for thirty
hours at least. Our food was assured and our lousy
bunks were ready.

The sun dazzled over green fields, running brooks
and distant hills in a section of the world that is
second to none in beauty. Morons, cynical and brutal and bewhipt of life many of us were, we responded to the passing beauty and our moods were
high.

Rosebud Bates had joined our group at the last
stop. He had friends in Jock and myself. No man

Circus Parade

dared to be uncivil with Jock. He was a man who would have shoved Napoleon off the road. A dozen years on the race tracks as exercise boy and later a famous jockey, a murder in his pocket, twenty years in a penitentiary, and his body a sieve for morphine, he was, nevertheless, a strong and humane person.

The horses would whinny when he drew near. He would talk to them as though they were people.

"They never double-cross you, kid, an' they give you more than they take. They call 'em dumb animals—it's people that's dumb—I know."

Among us was Goosey, the elephant trainer. He was a man in the middle thirties with no chin. His face was bent like a quarter moon in the middle. His nose was abnormally long and hooked. It hung over his mouth like a beak. He was sensitive to the touch of a human hand on any part of his anatomy. If a finger was laid upon his body unexpectedly he would jump several feet. We called him Goosey, a nickname given men of his type in our world. The men often teased him. Jock would allow no man to touch Goosey in his presence.

Another fellow had joined us the day before. He had worked hard, and was here, there and everywhere when we loaded the circus. He was about six feet tall, immensely proportioned, a heavy face with

Murder for Pity

deep hollows in his cheeks, and mouth which he closed like a vise. He had no coat. He wore a straw hat with half of the rim gone, and a heavy and greasy blue flannel shirt. Wide open at the throat, it showed a matted chest which the sun had burned a deep red. There was a battleship tattooed under the hair. He had the restless furtive look about his eyes which I early observed as a lad on the road —the eyes of men who never rested. Vagabonds all, their bodily and mental faculties may have been dead. But their eyes were always alert, quickly noting everything that pertained to ways of vagabondage—theft, destitution and dirt. The wolf learns cunning to survive; the vagabond observation. I could tell by his manner that he was old in the ways of the road.

There was another indescribable little man with us. He was more ordinary than a weed on a farm. So negative was he that across the years I can barely see the blur of him in a pair of overalls.

"Well this beats bummin' our way," said the last man, glancing across a green field.

"Maybe so, maybe so, but I'll jump the outfit before we hit where we're goin'," said the man with the tanned breast and blue flannel shirt. "The old road knocks hell outta you, but there hain't nobody your boss," he added, looking about him.

"Everybody's your boss when you're on the bum, Mate," laughed Jock, "every woman you beg and every cop you see."

Jock suddenly looked up at the sun. Three quarters down the sky, it drew many shafts of light from the clouded horizon, which made it resemble an immense half-wheel.

"God Almighty, ain't that great," he half-shouted. "Holy God," his head shook with wonder. "It's enough to drive you nuts." Jock shifted about nervously. I knew that the urge for morphine was upon him. He threw his head far back, then rolled it from side to side as if to rest the base of his brain.

He went to another part of the car and sat quite still.

The vagabond in the blue flannel shirt sang:

We are two tramps, two jolly old tramps,
We're happy as two Turks,
We have good luck in bummin' our chuck
An' to hell wit' the man that works.

Finishing the verse, he turned to me.

"You people played the South, didn't you?"

Murder for Pity

"Sure . . . we've been down through there," I answered.

"So've I. I just came from that way myself. It's damn hard ridin', brother. They hain't civilized down there yet." He rubbed his matted chest, then took off his torn straw hat and scratched his head. "They stuck me six months down there, by God, damn near killed me. Got me under the platform in the Montgomery freight yards on the L. & N. It was colder'n hell and the wind blew through your whiskers a mile and a half a minute. A hundred an' eighty days the judge soaked me—in a coal mine. I'd been in the navy, got soused in Birmingham an' some bloke rolled me for all the dough I had. I had nothin' on me at all. The desk sergeant books me on as D.S. (dangerous and suspicious), for I was a husky baby an' they needed guys for the coal mines.

"We were all lined up before the judge who was a cockeyed little pimple of a man, squirtin' tobacco juice all the time. He laughed in our faces, an' there was about twenty of us. He had the cops sort us out, the big guys, the medium guys an' the little guys. An' he says to about five of the biggest of us, 'You big fellows there, a hundred and eighty days each in the coal mines—hard labor. A hundred days for you medium guys—same thing. And you little guys'—an' I watched 'em all stand up like they was goin' to git off easy—'a hundred an' ninety days, cause you can't do as much work as the other hoboes.' The judge laughed out loud at his joke.

"I says under my breath, 'You dirty dog.' The cop says, 'What's that?' an' I thinks fast an' says, 'I was just figgerin' up how long I'd be in.' 'You'd better be,' says the cop."

The vagabond scratched his breast again.

"Some day I'll kill that God damn judge. I'll go roamin' through there wit' a gat an' shoot him at his table. He deserves a dose of lead to let the poison outta his black heart. I've been a bum all my life an' joined the navy to see the world when Roosevelt had the ships go round it. By God, all I did was shovel coal in four shifts an' was so damn tired when my relief come I couldn't even see outta the port hole. I beat it away from the damn navy at Frisco an' headed for New Orleans.

"I'd made too fast a time for them ever to get my mug up as a deserter. Believe me, boes, that join' the navy to see the world's like a wild woman dreamin' o' bein' tame. It just ain't done this year.

"Anyhow, I did the six months with another buddy. It drove him clean nuts. When he got out

Murder for Pity

he thought he was Andy Carnay-gie an' owned a steel mill, the poor devil. He kep' sayin' the day we got out, 'Get to work there, men, get to work there. There ain't nothin' like work boys, nothin' like work. An' save your money, boys, save your money. Andy Carnay-gie, that's me, always saved his money.' I had to walk along the tracks so damn weary my knees knocked together and listen to this poor goof rave."

We stopped at a siding. There was a lull. We heard a supper bell ringing far away.

"That bird's got it on us," said the indescribable vagrant. "He kin go in an' sit down to a warm feed an' sleep wit' a woman in clean sheets that hain't lousy. An' he kin pat his little wife in the mornin' an' she'll get up an' cook him some ham an' eggs—an' all's dandy for the day."

"Yeah, hell," snapped the man in the blue shirt, "he probably wishes he was us. Them damned clod-hoppers hain't no happier'n we are. They're like a lotta cows."

"Well, what happened to the nutty guy?" I asked as Jock joined us, his eyes dilated.

"Oh yeah," resumed the man quickly. "Well, sir, you know, the dark and all that—it ruins your eyes. Six months of it, you know, by God. Purple things

[87]

Circus Parade

begin to dance in front of you. I kep' mine closed
much as possible.

"Well, bein' up in the light the first day after
six months nearly drove him nuts besides." We all
looked quickly at each other as he went on. "I don't
claim to have any heart. It don't make a damn bit
of difference. I had a notion to bump him off myself
the first night. Then I changed my mind.

"He kep' askin' me, 'if I git nutty, bump me off,
won't you Buddy, afore Alabama gits me agin.
You'll be doin' me a big favor, honest you will.
They'd only kill me and give me to kid doctors to
cut up.'

"The next night he got worse an' set a store on
fire. I got him outta that scrape after knockin' him
cold by sloughin' him on the jaw an' carryin' him
four blocks to the railroad yards. I thought sure
I'd cracked him hard enough to put him out till
mornin'. So I snoozed off, and along about mornin'
I heard the damndest explosion in the world. It
shook me where I lay. I jumped up off the box-car
floor where we'd flopped, and my buddy was gone.
Right away I ran down the track in the direction of
a burnin' box car. The yards were light as day. I
saw a guy runnin' away out at the edge of the tracks
carryin' a torch. All of a sudden there was an-

Murder for Pity

other explosion an' I was knocked to the ground. I jumped up, and, by God, there was another blast, an' I don't know whether I was knocked down or just plain fell flat. But I got up again an' ran after the guy wit' the torch. It was my buddy. When he saw me comin' he yells:

" 'I'm gettin' even with the God damn state of Alabama. I'm runnin' to Montgomery to blow the damn judge up.'

"I kep' laughin' easy till I come up close to him. An' then I let him have it right on the point of the jaw. It knocked him cold an' the torch fell. I jumped on it quick an' put it out. Then I grabbed my buddy and took him a coupla hundred feet back of an old shed that was used to store cotton.

"My buddy left his shoes in the car, an' the explosion had scared me. An', by thunder, I left mine too—an' there we were both barefooted an' a lot of burnin' box cars makin' the yards lighter'n hell. His ankles were bleedin' from the chains that 'ad been on 'em six months, an' I was scared they might track him by the blood.

"As quick as I could get my noodle workin' I searched him.

"He had a blue gat shoved in his inside coat pocket, wit' three bullets outta the barrel. This

[89]

Circus Parade

scared the livin' hell right outta me. I knew if they caught me I'd swing for murder. I went off my nut for a minute an' thought I heard a lotta bloodhounds bayin' right outside. It all came to me in a flash. I'd remembered seein' a half dozen cars in the yards marked red on the cards tacked to 'em:

DANGEROUS
High Explosives
Keep Lights and Fires Away

I never thought my nutty buddy'd seen 'em, but he had. An' mind you, he was near blind. Then I tried to figger out where he got the gat. An' while I was sittin' there thinkin', I heard a noise outside.

"I gripped the gun an' decided to shoot it out with any damn cop before he let the air through me. Soon everything got quieter an' I sat there holdin' the gun till it got so damn still you could hear a cricket walk. I'd been through so damned much that I musta dozed off, but I woke up quick wit' somethin' snarlin' at me like a tiger. My arm was damn near broke across the wrist. My buddy'd cracked it wit' a club an' took the gun. I shoved in close to him so's he couldn't use it, an' just got

[90]

Murder for Pity

inside in time to push it down an' she went off between my left armpit an' my side. It stunned me for a second, an' the old boy grabbed me by the throat an' my tongue popped out. I thought I was a goner. I'm strong enough to knock a bull down, but that nutty old buddy o' mine had me comin' in second. He was after my throat an' I was after the gun. Everything went black for a second, an' I thought faster . . ."

The man with the matted chest stopped talking and sighed. Jock lit a kerosene lantern and hung it on a nail a few feet above the floor.

The man felt his throat nervously and resumed:

"Anyhow I'd made up my mind that if I was man enough to twist the gun around an' pull the trigger on my nutty buddy I'd put him outta his misery, as it was him or me anyhow. Besides, if they'd of got him they'd of hung him or somethin', an' he was too nutty to do that with. So I just couldn't help havin' pity for him.

"But I never saw anything so strong. His muscles were like a lion's an' my left arm was goin' numb on me before I twisted the gun aroun' back of his ear an' the bullet zipped through his head like hot water through a pipe. It came out under his left

Circus Parade

eye and scraped my cheek and knocked me kickin'!"

"Lordy! Lordy!!" exclaimed Goosey, "it's a wonder you ain't nutty yourself."

"Ye—ap, it is a won—der," drawled the prisoner from Alabama.

"How'd you make the getaway?" Jock asked, with roused interest.

"God I don't know. A fellow never knows how he does those things. I stuck my buddy between two old cotton bales. I thought I was headin' north, but got all balled up an' headed in the direction of Pensacola. I musta beat it fifteen miles without stoppin'—right across country wit' no more shoes than a rabbit before I climbed up in a big pine tree an' slep' there. Then I had to backtrack after I watched the sun a minute 'cause I wanted to go north.

"That night I hit a nigger settlement. They give me some old shoes and some things an' let me sleep in their shack, an' they never woke me for a day and a half. I'd slep' that long. Finally, an old grey-headed nigger took me in a peddler wagon to the Junction, an' I caught a freight for Birmingham."

VI: Tales are Told

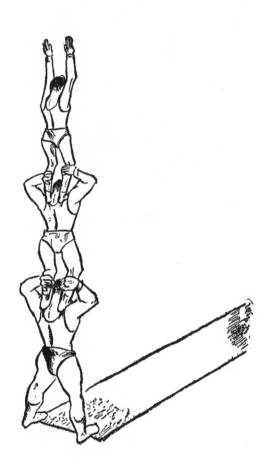

VI: Tales are Told

A SOLEMN silence followed the man's tale. We all sat very still and looked straight ahead. Jock rose and seated himself between me and the man who had killed his comrade.

The murderer for pity sat with clenched jaws, a look of madness in his eyes. Jock touched him on the arm. He jumped and reached for his hip pocket.

"That's all right, old scout. You don't need to mind me, I'm all O. K." Jock paused. "But I'd never tell that yarn again if I were you. You'll bump into some guy on the road who'll turn you in for a plugged nickel."

The man's jaws opened suddenly. "I don't give a damn. I'll bang the buttons off any damn bull that comes near me. I'm willin' to burn in the chair to kill a few cops an' that judge in Alabama."

Jock's voice went easy. We all listened attentively. "But after you kill 'em all, then what?" he asked.

Jock laughed in his throat, and continued:

"You know, old boy, you ain't been through it

Circus Parade

all. A lot o' guys have been in longer'n six months in a coal mine." He laughed in his throat again. "Christ Almighty, man, that's only one night compared to a twenty-year jolt."

We stopped at a junction point.

"Where the hell are we?" someone asked.

"Some little jerk-water place," I answered. "The Missouri Pacific crosses here." We looked out and saw the white tops of two steel rails stretch toward the southwest.

We could hear the restless moving of the elephants in the car ahead.

Over the sudden stillness came the dismal whining of a hyena. "It's funny about those damn things," said Goosey, "they know more about the weather than the Lord himself. That whine means rain within two days. You can't fool 'em. Their whine's different when it's goin' to turn cold. They howl louder an' they start all the other animals doin' the same." He held up his hand as the noise became louder. "You see, some more've started. Them's the two in the cage with the blind brown bear." Suddenly other members of the cat family began howling. Then quickly it subsided.

The sky was blue and purple in the west.

The engine could be heard taking long tired

Tales are Told

breaths of steam. The elephants still stamped nervously.

The murderer for pity, jaws unmoving, stared into the darkness.

"More rain," said a voice. "It's the wettest year I ever seen with the tents."

The air turned murky and heavy. Frogs croaked along the track. We listened to them for several minutes.

"Well," said Goosey at last, "I think I'll step up an' see how my big babies are makin' it." He jumped out of the car and went toward the elephants.

"Think I'll take a little walk too," said the prisoner from Alabama. He pushed his torn straw hat low on his head, jumped to the ground quickly and walked toward the Missouri Pacific tracks.

I watched him until he could be seen no more.

Often I have wondered what became of him, and who he was, and from where. With the code of the road, we asked no questions. He had volunteered much. Like most rovers he had said nothing about his identity. He did not return.

Goosey came back to our car. The train moved on.

"It's hell, a guy like that runnin' around loose," said Jock, his mind still with the man who had gone.

Circus Parade

"He'll bump somebody off just as sure's there's noise in dynamite." Jock whistled and then laughed. "Oh well, I should worry a lot an' build a house. It's no pansies off my grave. But I wouldn't wanta be that judge in Alabama."

"I hope to hell he gets him," volunteered the indescribable man.

"Me too," said Goosey, "he deserves it."

"Yes, an' every other judge, an' the lawyers too —and the cops—kill 'em all, the damn bloody bloodsuckers, that's my motto," sneered Jock.

"Don't you want no law in the world?" asked the indescribable man.

"Law? What the hell's the good of it?" leered Jock. "If they'd put everybody in jail that's out, an' let everybody out that's in, we'd be just as well off. Them on the outside's the biggest crooks. They're smooth enough to keep out," he said with finality.

"But wasn't he a big guy, though. He was tall as Denna Wyoming," I said, in an effort to veer Jock's mind.

"Yeap," laughed Jock, "poor old Denna. It took a lot of clean dirt to cover him. I'll never forget the time he saved Bad Bill the lion from dyin' of pneumonia. He put mustard plasters a yard long

[98]

on him, an' now the vicious devil's up there howlin' an' Denna's in his grave." He sighed. "Old Cameron sure cashed in big when he died."

"He was a good fellow," said Whiteface.

"None better in the world," responded Jock.

"He sure knew how to handle animals," put in Goosey. "One time when Cameron got that lion with a lotta boils, Denna just quit feedin' it fat an' it got all right agin. He'd never feed the lions on Sunday. Makin' 'em fast one day was good for 'em. He'd only give the lions meat an no fat—an' a big bunch. He used to say a little meat was worse'n none at all."

"Poor old Denna," Jock said, half reminiscently, "he could hold more licker than a copper tank an' never show it. I'll never forget the time Bad Bill got loose on top of the cage—remember that, Goosey?" Turning to me, he said, "That was before you joined us, kid. Well you know—the lion used to ride on top the cage lyin' down. It was chained so fas' to the top it couldn't get up. But the rubes couldn't see the chains. They thought it was just lyin' there peaceful. Six girls used to ride right around him; sittin' there easy like. An' all the rubes seein' the parade pass by would think how brave they were.

Circus Parade

"Well one time Denna's helper forgot to chain Bill, or else he got loose. Bill stood up an' looked around right where the crowd was the thickest. The Strong Woman saw the lion git up and damn near fell off on her head. The Moss-Haired Girl just says under her breath like to the five others:

" 'Just sit real quiet. Maybe he'll think he's chained an' lie down again.' The Strong Woman and the rest of the girls jist sit there clenchin' their hands. Bad Bill stood up for a block or two, an' sure enough he musta thought he was still chained. He sniffed the floor like a cat an' lay right down agin an' never moved till we got back to the lot.

"Old Cameron was so tickled at the Moss-Haired Girl's nerve he tried to hug her. 'How'd you ever come to think so fast?' he asked her.

" 'It wasn' anything,' she says right back. 'Denna always told me never to let one of the big cats know I was afraid of it. I just remembered, that's all.' "

"But I've seen Denna nervous-like. Was he really brave?" I asked.

"I've always thought he was the bravest kind of a guy," answered Jock. "He knew he was takin' chances but he kep' right on. A boob never knows when he's takin' a chance. A brave man's a coward lots of times, jist like a lion."

Tales are Told

He paused, and then added with more verve, "Well, if Bad Bill ever tangles with Royal Bengal he'll get his'n. There can't no lion lick a tiger."

"Yeah, dey kin," said Whiteface.

Ignoring the shift in conversation, Goosey commented, "It's jist like an elephant or a lion. They hain't always brave. I guess it's 'cordin' to how their liver's workin'. I'll never forgit the time when I was wit' the Wallace shows. An elephant reached out its trunk and got hold of the Sacred Bull from India's tail and give it a hell of a yank while he was paradin'. That bull roared like old Mahomend himself and rares on his hind legs like he ain't use to such famelarity." Goosey laughed. "But you shoulda seen the keeper. He was one of them Mohamends too. He jumped right up in the air an' grabbed the elephant's ear an' started beatin' him over the head wit' his whip. That elephant woulda killed any other guy in the world but that Mahomend. He jist lay right down an' took the beatin' like he knowed he'd done somethin' unholy. Then I comes up an' he sees me an' gits his nerve back an' Mahomend starts to run towards his bull. But he only gits 'bout four feet when mister elephant reaches out his trunk easy like and ketches him around the neck. It gives him a little flip an' up he goes in the air like a

Circus Parade

bird an' down he comes like a ton o' brick an' lights
right on the back of mister bull from India. Well,
sir, youda thought it 'ud caught Mahomend shootin'
craps. It jist bellered an' stuck its head an' started
to run an' it darn near busted up the parade. You
see, them bulls 're saccerd. They've been blessed by
the Pope or somethin' an' they hain't used to elephants pullin' their tails 'er havin' people light on
their back that way. But you see how that elephant
wasn't brave at first."

The tale of the Sacred Bull had amused Whiteface. He laughed often, his white teeth showing dis-
tinctly in the uneven light.

"That reminds me," said the Indescribable One,
"of the time I was on the bum wit' a venterliquist.
They was passin' the collection box in church when
he throws his voice up behin' the altar an' says to
the preacher, 'Who the hell told you that you was
right, you old fathead? Look at me. I'm your God
up in the ceilin'. An' all the rubes look up, an' he
takes the collection box an' walks outta the church
wit' it, me followin' after him. That preacher darn
near sits down right there. You see it got him when
his liver wasn't good or somethin'. You're right,
Jock, them things do happen. Anyhow we beats it
to a restaurant and after we has two big beefsteaks

[102]

Tales are Told

my buddy he says to me, 'Now that you gotta chance you'd better eat enough for tomorrow.'

" 'God! I'll say I will,' I says, 'but gimme time. I hain't et enough for yisterday yit.' "

Everybody laughed while the engine whistled five times to call in the flagman.

The car, in spite of the open door, became nauseating. The heavy air did not move swiftly enough to carry the many odors of the circus away from the track.

"I wish the train 'ud move. The damn circus don't smell so bad when we're runnin'," said Jock.

"Smoke cigarettes like I do," advised the Indescribable One, "then you can't smell it so much."

Soon several cigarettes were lit.

"Some one done tell me we was goin' furder away daown south?" Whiteface, the tall Negro in the group, asked anxiously.

"Yeap, that's so Whiteface. We're circlin' through Arkansas, then over through another part of Lousiana till we hit the gulf, so they tell me," Jock volunteered. "But don't you never mind."

"Well it do make some neber mind to me, say what you don't please no time."

The worried expression soon left the Negro's face and he whistled his favorite verse:

Circus Parade

My masteh had a yaller gal,
An' she was frum the Souf;
Her hair it kinked so berry tight,
She coulden shut her mouf.

He laughed musically. "Ah'se dreamin' last night ah'se a big white buhd a flyin' aroun', an' somebody squirts lotta ink on me. Wasen dat a funny dream?"

The giant Negro's carefree manner had made me his friend. "I'll say it was, Whiteface." The Negro sat very still with a wide smile on his face.

"Talkin' about dreams, Whiteface," said Jock, "let me tell you one I heard from an acrobat who'd been over'n England wit' Barnum. It sure knocked me for a loop an' I can't forget it."

"Dat so—dat so?" And the Negro smiled anxiously.

"It's about three people dreamin' the same thing at the same time." Jock looked keenly at Whiteface.

"Do *tell*," pleaded the Negro.

"Well now you gotta get it straight," and Jock addressed himself to Whiteface as if he were the only one in the audience. "This acrobat's wife lived down near Buffalo an' she'd never seen the ocean— remember that."

[104]

Tales are Told

"Ah will," the Negro answered quickly, and leaned forward as though his life depended on every word.

"Well this acrobat took a low black steamer home. It was crowded as the devil and he had to share a room with another guy. He was homesick to see his wife and he went to bed thinkin' about her. There was a big storm and the boat rolled all over the ocean before he finally got to sleep. The guy over'n the other bed was snorin' like an Erie freight engine by that time.

"When the acrobat did get to sleep he dreamt his wife came into the room and stood still for a minute when she saw another guy asleep across from her man. She held her hands together and at last got up nerve to go over to her husband and tuck him in and then kiss him goodnight. Nervous-like, she looked over to the guy who was still snorin' and hurried outta the room."

Jock paused for a long effect.

"Is dat all?" asked Whiteface impatiently.

"I'll say it ain't," replied Jock much pleased. "It ain't even the starter."

"Go on, go on," said Whiteface.

Jock smiled crookedly.

Circus Parade

"Well when both the guys woke up in the mornin' and started dressin', the snorin' guy says to the acrobat:

" 'You're a dandy, havin' a good lookin' Jane come into the room and hug an' kiss you. I laid there hopin' she'd come over an' give me a smack.'

"The acrobat was so surprised you coulda knocked him over wit' a feather.

" 'What did the woman look like?' he asked his room mate.

"You coulda knocked him over wit' half a feather when the guy described the acrobat's wife to him.

" 'My God,' he yells. An' all that trip he'd not go near the other fellow. He had his room changed an' everything. He thought he was a devil.

"When the acrobat got to New York he took a train for the burg near Buffalo. His wife said to him right away, 'Dear, you had a stormy voyage at first, didn't you?'

" 'Yes,' he said. 'How'd you know, sweetheart?'

" 'Well the first night I knew you were leavin' Liverpool I dreamt it was awful stormy and your little low black boat was rockin' about as if it would be washed under any minute.

" 'I was dreadfully frightened and hurried to your state-room. I got half way in before I saw a

[106]

Tales are Told

man sleepin' in the other bed. I stopped in the middle of the floor and gathered my courage together and went over and tucked you in and kissed you goodnight. The man was so strange lookin' that I was scared of him and hurried out.'

" 'What did he look like?" her husband asked.

"An' the acrobat's wife described the guy in the state-room she had never seen only in a dream. She'd never seen the boat either for that matter and she had it down pat too."

Jock paused and looked at Whiteface. His eyes were larger than usual. The smile had been routed by a more serious expression.

"Lawdy! Lawdy! dat suah am spooky. What kinda licker dem folks drinkin' nohow?"

Jock laughed. "No kind at all, Whiteface. The brain's a funny thing. Just think how them three people saw the same thing at the same time. I'll say the brain's funny."

"My brain ain't dat funny, Misteh Jock. An' what's some moah I woan habe no brain 'tall if eveh I heahs many moah tales like dat one."

"You're sure right, Whiteface. I think we'd all better hit the hay on that yarn," laughed Goosey.

"When'll we strike?" I asked.

"About eight in the morning. We'll parade be-

[107]

Circus Parade

fore noon. Everybody ought to be feelin' fine for the long rest—except old Cameron and the Baby Buzzard. They'll surely jerk in the nickels tomorrow," laughed Jock, "so I'll pound my ear and you fellows can do what you like."

We slept while our weird caravan rattled over the ties.

VII: Without What?

VII: Without What?

WE arrived in ——, Arkansas, completely
rested and in high spirits.

Cameron walked about the lot after the tent was
up and rubbed his hands gleefully. Slug Finnerty,
his one eye now open, prepared his blue ticket
wagon early. Rosebud and the other musicians prac-
ticed in their tent. The Strong Woman sang *Die
Wacht am Rhein*, while a few stray "rubes" stood
outside her little tent and listened.

Goosey had his three elephants ready for parade
early. One of his helpers, a boy like myself, had
deserted the circus. Some one always rode each elephant in parade. Cameron ordered me to ride in the
boy's place. Goosey rigged me out in an Arab cos-
tume.

"Arabs don't ride elephants, Goosey, do they?"
I asked.

"They do wit' this circus, kid," he answered.
"That's the only outfit we got left."

The ragged roustabouts with the circus would
immediately feel all-important once they donned

Circus Parade

the vari-colored uniforms for parade. But the lice bit viciously beneath their gaudy apparel, and often, though clad in sumptuous regalia, our minds were on lesser things.

News of our hey rube battle had not reached this section. The lot was crowded with people.

As I stood near the elephant with Goosey, who was ready to place me on its back, Cameron approached.

"We'll clean up a lotta money today, Goosey," he smiled, and walked on.

"He means he'll clean up the money, the old bum. All I'll do is clean up after the elephants. The old cuss is just castrated wit' joy when he makes a lotta money." And Goosey frowned as he put his animals in line for parade.

We made a triumphant tour of the town. We returned to the lot where a huge crowd awaited us. The midway was crowded.

Our "world's champion" high diver had just hurled himself from an eighty foot ladder into a small tank of water. He came out dripping and shivering. A lithe-limbed boy stood on his hands atop a red wagon. His body formed a curve. The crowd applauded. Climbing down he saw the flag on the cook-tent and hurried away to his dinner.

Without What?

The snake-charmer waved a rock python about while the spieler clanged on an iron triangle to draw the crowd. His place was quickly taken by a swarthy fellow who pounded a huge drum with his hand. He was joined by a darker chap who played a terrifying tune on a weird clarinet. Then Socrates Whipper, the spieler, appeared again.

He beamed the benevolence of a country minister. He looked like a man who had a world to save. A black string tie was crooked on his "come to Jesus" collar. A ring made out of a horseshoe nail was on the third finger of his left hand. He held the thumb of it in his vest. A large Elk tooth, colored green, hung from a heavy gold chain stretched across his vest. There was a look of sadness about his eyes. Strangely enough, they danced with humor when he smiled. His lower jaw was longer than daylight, and moved swiftly. His words were as smooth as an egg in wine. He was saying:

"Lefita, the favorite dancer of the Sultan, who escaped the horrors of a Turkish harem and was brought to this country by the generous owners of this circus to present for you the secret dances of Egypt. She knows the lure of the dances of the world. She it was who danced for the kings of im-

Circus Parade

potent glory. E-v-e-r-y mu-s-cl-e-e-v-e-ry-fib-er in this little la-dees ana-tom-ee quiver-s and shakes like an aspen leaf in a gale of wind-or like a bowl of jell-ee, gentle*men*-on a cold and frost-ee morning. She makes the old feel young and the young feel gay, the blind to see and cripples to throw their crutches away."

Lefita appeared behind the benevolent-looking spieler and gave a body quiver that started at her feet and rolled upward. Her copper-colored form was fascinating. It moved with the poetry of motion as she walked away.

"The little lady will retire. The show will start immediately. All will be out and over before the big show commences. There are three ticket boxes —tickets a quarter, twenty-five cents. You will see the little people, the pygmies, the Bearded Lady, and Amy. The wonderful Amy weighs seven hundred and ninety pounds, and yet is as dainty as any of her sisters. You will see the sword swallower, the glass blowers from Bohemia, and many dangerous reptiles in a glass-enclosed den. All for twenty-five cents."

As the din died away the listeners filed inside. Shadows danced across the trampled grass within. Green flies buzzed about mournfully.

[114]

Without What?

The Moss-Haired Girl, the Strong Woman and other freaks, having just returned from the cook-tent, were mounting their stands and arranging photographs, which they sold. The sword-swallower wiped her nickle-plated weapon with a soft cloth. The snake-charmer confided to Bosco, the wild man, her worry about a sinuous pet.

"He's got a canker in his mouth and I've touched it with caustic and washed it with bismuth but it just don't seem to do no good. He's due to eat next month and I'm worried as all hell. I hope it'll be well by then."

She looked concerned toward the wild man, who advised:

"Lemme tell you. Jest clean it out a weeny teeny bit and put a midgie piece o' saltpeter on it. That'll fix it up. I did that with a big anaconda for Millie Delay when I was a spieler for the Sparks show."

The benevolent-looking spieler followed the crowd inside and went from one platform to another until he came to the far end where stood the charming Lefita. He beamed beside her.

A crowd of men stood in front of them. Of all ages, with expressions of sex-wonder in their eyes, gazing curiously as men will who cannot solve a mystery that populates graveyards and through the

Circus Parade

ages has sent poets, popes, kings and fools to the junk-heap.

The drum throbbed. The clarinet shrieked. Lefita shivered languidly. The music became more violent and Lefita's body kept in tune. It moved like something boneless but sensuous.

The movement ended in a gyration that seemed to leave her exhausted. It was a short dance. The onlookers stood curious and expectant. The spieler then called them closer and said blandly, "I recognize some real sports amongst you, gentlemen, with good red blood coursing through your corpuscles. But would you like it, gentlemen, if this little lady would put on a special show for you? She just told me inside that she had never seen so many handsome men—and the young lady sees a great many."

The center of the young lady's body moved sensuously.

"Sure! Sure! Sure!!" yelled a chorus of shillabers. (A shillaber is a herder of suckers.) They were noisy in eagerness.

"Go easy, gentlemen," admonished the spieler, "we mustn't overstep the bounds of the conventions. The young lady is very temperamental and loud demonstrations interfere with her body movements."

The shillabers were still insistent.

Without What?

"No, wait a moment, gentlemen," said the spieler as he stopped to plead with Lefita, who hung her head, pouting, her splendid body moving the while as she shook her head coyly and disappeared. The shillabers made another demonstration in which the other onlookers joined.

"Of course, gentlemen, there will be an extra charge for this—just a thin silver dollar apiece—and of course all that we collect will go to the little lady herself. The little girl will be glad to give the special engagement for you. Move closer boys, move closer." He made a motion with his hand. "Listen, if you boys ever had that funny feeling—*you know*—she'll give it to you as you've never had it before. You know the Sultan of Turkey and the King of England's each got a lot of wives and seeing women is of course no preponderant mystery to them, but they got a rise out of Lefita. . . ."

The shillabers pushed forward, carrying the crowd with them.

"Don't crowd, folks. Remember always that you are American gentlemen," said the spieler.

Then a shillaber's voice boomed:

"I say, Professor, I wonder if she'll give that doniker dance she put on over in Emoryville the other night."

Circus Parade

The spieler rubbed his hands, puzzled.

"Oh you mean that special show we put on at the Elks' lodge?"

"Yep, that's it," answered the shillaber.

"Well, you boys are hot sports all right. I'll go in and ask her if she will. But of course, in all fairness, it should cost fifty cents more apiece."

The men eagerly awaited the return of the spieler. While he was gone the shillaber who had asked for the doniker dance described in a loud voice the dance he had seen at the Elks' blowout.

The spieler returned with a cautious expression.

"There are no police amongst you, is there?"

Many voices answered in unison:

"No!"

"Well," he went on, "the little lady said she'd do it all right. It's very trying, you know, you never saw such a movement. Lord, what passion! But, as I say, it will cost fifty cents extra, a small dollar and a half. A show the like of which you'll never see this side of heaven again."

Another shillaber clapped his hands loudly.

"What do you say, gentlemen, if we all chip in another half dollar and give it to the lady. Two little silver dollars ain't much and look what a show

Without What?

we'll see. We may as well be real sports. We don't
see things like this every day, and I'm for helpin'
the little girl. We've all got sisters and mothers
and they've got to git along. And if we gentlemen
don't help them, who will?" Two other shillabers
cried, "Here's my two dollars."

One after another several dozen race perpetua-
tors handed the spieler the required amount. After
he had collected from the last one, he pulled aside a
flap of canvas and let the men pass into what seemed
to be an adjoining tent.

There was a platform inside upon which Lefita
did not stand. Fearful music was made upon the
drum and clarinet.

"Say, Professor," spoke up a shillaber when the
music ceased, "now that we're in here *you* be a good
sport. What's the matter with having the little lady
do the dance—*without—you know!*"

The spieler looked concerned and cautious at the
same time. He held up a long smooth hand. "Why,
boys, I can't ask her to do that. Gracious, gentlemen, this is too much. You should have told me before I let you in here that you wanted the whole
show. Why she got five dollars apiece from the
Elks last week for putting that on. Sometimes the
Shriners give her even ten dollars apiece." He

looked about, then spoke softly. "But wait, I'll ask her."

He was gone for a moment.

"Gosh, I wish she'd do it *without*. Boy, O boy— she's got a knockout form. Anna Held's a blue jay compared to her. Zowie, she'd make Julius Seezar a bum over night. I never saw nothin' like her over to the Elks," said a shillaber.

The dazed members of the stronger sex looked at the speaker as the spieler returned.

"She doesn't want to do it for that price, boys, and you can't much blame her. She's a modest young lady and it's a very trying dance. Just think, as lovely as young Eve in the Garden. Think of it, gentlemen, and be lenient. As I say, she got five dollars last week over at the Elks."

"Oh well, come on," said a shillaber impatiently. "Let's all give another dollar and have the whole works."

The men trembled in anticipation as the spieler raised his hand and said:

"Yes, gentlemen, I'll be fair. One dollar more each and I'll see that she gives the whole show— the Egyptian dance, the doniker dance, and the wonderful dance *without*. Think of it, gentlemen, the soul-stirring—the voluptuous—the sensuous—

[120]

Without What?

the wonderful—the maddening dance *without*."
They all rushed forward with another dollar.

"Thank you, thank you, thank you, gentlemen,"
said the spieler as Lefita came through a side wall
and climbed upon the platform. She danced indifferently, her body moving slowly. In a short time
she disappeared.

"That was just the introduction, gentlemen,
merely a warming up of her lovely body. In a few
minutes she will do the dance without." He held
his long smooth hand up again. "Will all you gentlemen please remove your hats?" he said.

They did as they were told.

Lefita appeared and danced again in the same
apparel.

A shillaber sneered as Lefita bowed. *"Without
what?"* he yelled gruffly.

"Without your hats on," came the bland voice
of the spieler.

Suddenly the side-walls dropped and the aston-
ished spectators found themselves standing in the
open air.

They looked at each other sheepishly and melted
into the crowd.

The clarinet and the drum again played fearful
music.

Circus Parade

Lefita rested. The show closed for twenty minutes until other rubes had gathered. Finnerty's voice could be heard.

"Here you are, ladees and gentlemen. Tickets for the great and only—the great and only—I say the great and only Cameron's great combined shows just returned from tours of China and Japan and other points in the Far West. Be very, very careful, gentlemen. We try to run a respectful show, but beware of pickpockets. Guard your purses."

Socrates Whipple again appeared before Lefita's tent.

"She is the favorite dancer of the Sultan, ladies and gentlemen. She escaped the horrors of his harem and was brought to this country by the generous owners of this circus for your edification in the secret dances of Egypt."

And thus the farce was renewed.

By using every device possible through Arkansas, Cameron and his band soon recouped their losses.

Plundering and stealing, cheating and lying, laboring, fighting and loving; taking all we could and returning little, we went our careless and irresponsible ways, with laughter in our hearts and sneers on our lips—as anti-social as the hyenas who howled at the changes in the weather.

VIII: The Strong Woman

VIII : The Strong Woman

SHE weighed four hundred pounds. Her neck, shoulders and arms bulged with muscle. Her torso was set on hips far broader than her shoulders. Her small head was covered with short curly flaxen hair that seemed continually damp. It looked as out of place on her mountain of body as a small knob on an immense potato. Her feet were usually spread apart as if in readiness for some impending shock. They were covered with pink sandals and fastened with silk ribbons about her giant ankles. The circus billed her as "The Female Hercules, The Strongest Lady in the World." The flamboyant posters showed her as a young Juno with a face as placid as Queen Victoria's.

Her face was not without attraction. Her eyes were blue and beautiful. They stared sadly at a world without understanding. She had a red moist underlip that trembled with suppressed hurt. She would toss her head saucily as if to show the world that she was feminine, with the hopes and dreams and longings of her sex.

Circus Parade

Twenty-five years before she had first opened her eyes in a Hanoverian village. She was christened Lila. Life laughed at her kindly parents when the baby grew out of all proportions. At the age of twelve she could carry her father and mother. At thirteen she began to support the entire family as a weight lifter.

She came to America at the age of sixteen and first appeared in a Chicago Museum on South State street. After investing heavily in photographs, which did not sell, she broke her contract. The manager, a waspy little Greek, objected. She twisted his neck until he yelled for mercy in Greek and English. She then tore through the Museum like a raging elephant and left demolished paraphernalia all about her.

She joined out as a side show attraction with a traveling circus, and soon prospered. It was not long until she began to clothe herself in the fluffiest of dresses and the widest and most beribboned of hats. She imprisoned her body in the strongest of stays, and did everything to make herself as dainty as her little sisters.

Longing for love, she became an omnivorous reader of romance. Always scattered about her were paper-backed novels in German and English. They

The Strong Woman

were worlds into which her tired soul escaped. Her lips would move constantly as she read. Every now and then a little sigh would escape her. It would be followed with a heavier sigh at the end of each chapter. She would wipe her blue eyes often at the impassioned words uttered by the hero. She would be out of patience at the vacillations of the heroine who could not recognize true love in the first few chapters. When the book had been finished and hero and heroine had been united in joy forever, she would shake her perspiring flaxen head slowly and wipe her eyes, then pat the cover of the book as if it were the cheek of a child. "Ach Gott! How Beeootiful. How Sfeet." She would lay the book down gently and pick up another which told the same story in much the same way.

Lila had her dreams. And they were not of the circus, but always of the man who would come. She wanted to make sure and recognize him when he did. She often talked of him. At such times she would become shy and circumspect. But deep in her heavy breast a great urge was pounding.

She was wealthy as circus people go. She had a bundle of express money orders as big as her arm. Besides, she carried a "grouch bag" containing two thousand dollars. A grouch bag is usually carried suspended by a cord around the neck. It might be called the reserve bank of the circus rover. Lila often loaned money on proper security and with adequate interest. And often, though she became offended if anyone mentioned it, she gave money to those in need.

Life soon turned a page for Lila. On it were written many things.

The five Padronis sent for a new top-mounter to form the pinnacle of their human pyramid act. He left a stranded outfit to finish the season with us.

When Lila first saw Anton the world stood still for a moment. It then turned to chaos. He was the man. The great strong woman's body became limp and flabby at sight of him. She was filled with an ineffable longing. Everything seemed different. She gave me five dollars to run an errand for her. She was a heroine in one of her paper-backed novels. She bought more finery—and shoes that hurt her feet. She began to wear a vivid red ribbon across her forehead. She also purchased two yards of fancy material with which to make new garters.

Anton sat at a table across from her in the cook house. She always watched him, fascinated. He was lithe, delicate, and furtive-eyed. Curly knots of brown hair formed at the nape of his neck. Lila

[128]

The Strong Woman

made a mental photograph of him every day. She filled it with details of her own which she had garnered from the paper-back novels.

Alas, poor Lila, the pity of life and the wonder —the owls that would be eagles, and Amazons that would be sylphs.

Anton once played with his food as Lila watched. He felt superior to the fare placed in front of him. "The poor thing," thought Lila, "maybe he's sick." She called the waiter and said, "Tell the chef to give you some of mine chicken unt to slice it up nice." The waiter started toward the kitchen, nonplussed, when Lila called, "Give it to the nice-lookin' man sidding over there," pointing to Anton.

When the waiter placed the chicken in front of Anton, he looked up in surprise. When told that Lila had donated the delicacy, he bowed toward her.

Lila's heart pumped faster.

"Who is the fat heifer?" he asked the waiter.

"Oh she's the Female Hercules. She works in the side show. She ain't a bad egg," replied the waiter.

"Not half bad," commented Anton. "Good chicken, too."

Though contacts between those who work in the side show and those who listen to the applause of the big top is always limited, they soon became

Circus Parade

friends. When they first shook hands Anton expected crushed fingers. Instead, Lila's handshake was so gentle it would not have crushed a rose-leaf. And when Anton smiled at Lila half in ridicule, it filled her whole life with joyful madness. She would look in his eyes and forget she was the Female Hercules. The starved woman's soul in her fluttered and sang. When she turned away from Anton he would laugh sardonically. A woman in love is not an analyst. Else, whom would she marry? Her eyes held a soft light and her mammoth breast filled with desire to embrace the world at thought of Anton.

Trained to see the love-hunger of women, Anton made swift love to Lila. She responded, of course, as was her destiny.

She became more valuable to the side show; surpassing all previous efforts in weight lifting. Once, after Anton had petted her, she lifted eleven New York farmers and one editor.

With increasing strength came increasing dreams. She pictured herself in a little white-tiled German kitchen in the valley of the Rhine. She would sing to herself as she prepared food for Anton. She saw a garden with cabbages, kohlrabbi, carrots and onions, and white geese swimming on the river. She

The Strong Woman

saw Anton, the master, riding a black stallion over their farm. And often as she dreamed a voice would break in on her reverie—"Inside, ladies an' gentlemen, is the Female Hercules, the strongest woman in the world."

Lila was a real woman and not subtle. She told Anton how much money she had saved. All unaware she immediately became more attractive to him.

The top-mounter never had money. The dice game in the stake and chain wagon was the principal reason. He owed five hundred dollars to Buddy Conroy, who operated the game. He had promised to pay so much each time the ghost walked. But he had not paid. Anton always expected to win a great sum at each game. Just why is quite unfathomable. Conroy was at the head of an able crew. Any of them could take a pair of dice and roll the scale —from two to twelve and back again. They would shoot dice all summer on the road and work in Chicago gambling houses during the winter.

And once Lila saw Anton dining with Marie, the bareback rider, who was slender and beautiful. She returned to her tent with heart as heavy as her body and picked up a paper-backed novel. She tried to read for a long time. Her blue eyes blurred.

"It be not fair," she sobbed. "It be not fair."

Circus Parade

She tore the book in two and walked to the mirror. "Mein Gott," she wailed, "you be not good to me."

That agony passed quickly. For no woman was ever a realist long.

Lila soon had dreams again.

While the days merged into fall Anton was a busy person. He was winning with Lila and losing with Conroy. Somehow he never seemed able to pay Conroy anything. Lila had loaned him small sums which he always forced her to take back.

"No gentleman would take money for keeps from a woman, Lila, my little dear," he would tell her. And once again Lila saw angels throwing roses from the sky.

It was the last pay-day before the circus closed. All wanted to win money for the winter. Excitement ran high.

"Now listen, Mounter, I want you to pay me after the game if you win," said Conroy as he winked at a pal.

"All right, I will," answered Anton. "I feel lucky today."

Anton was really lucky at first. Then a pair of loaded dice entered the game. He lost four times in a row. The last pass took every cent he had.

The Strong Woman

After it was over Conroy said, "Listen Guy, you had your chance. Now'f you don't pay me before the show closes, I'll have the gang beat you up. See!"

"I'll pay you, Buddy. Just give me time."

"Well you better," returned Conroy.

Anton wandered down the midway thinking of Lila. As he approached her stand inside the tent, she gave him a warm smile.

"Say listen, Lila. I've got something *very important* to talk to you about," he said, as the band blared outside. "Can I see you tonight, Girlie?"

Lila's heart leaped. She could hardly control herself.

"Why—why—yes—come right here after the show," she said, ecstatically.

"All right, Lila," replied Anton, a happy lilt in his voice.

"What a cinch," he thought as he went to his dressing-room.

The evening dragged slowly for Lila. When the last show was over she hurried to her tent. She took her usual rub-down with more energy and then bathed herself with eau-de-cologne. She then dressed in her finest garments.

With trembling fingers she fastened snaps and

Circus Parade

tied bows. The big moment of her life was rapidly approaching. She listened joyfully to the band playing in the big show. She could tell by the number being played how far the show had advanced. It would not be long now till the finale. The races were now on. She must hurry. She floundered, rhinoceros like, about the tent. She looked in the mirror and for the tenth time dabbed powder on her face.

She then sat down on a specially-built canvas chair and tried to compose herself. All the drowned emotions of her life bubbled to the surface. She felt like singing. Twice she rose and looked out through the tent flap.

Then, as if to control her joy, she sang some melancholy German lines:

> *And if the stars in heaven*
> *My sufferings could know,*
> *Their light would soon be given*
> *To lessen of my woe.*

> *But none of them can know it—*
> *One only knows my pain;*
> *And only him could do it*
> *Has rent my heart in twain. . . .*

The Strong Woman

Her heavy voice boomed through the little tent as a sudden burst of wind flapped the covers of her paper-backed novels.

"Something very important"—her mind clung to the words. Then dreams again, more dreams, a long honeymoon. Maybe she'd just work at the fairs and let Anton run the little farm. Maybe she wouldn't have to lift so many farmers on a plank at the fairs—three or four would be enough. That would be easy. And it didn't make no difference if the place wasn't on the Rhine. America was plenty good with Anton. A chicken coop chuck full of white hens. She closed her eyes and held her head backward.

Resting her great hands on the arms of the canvas chair, she sat quite still, her mountainous body dressed in delicate finery. Through her flaxen head roved dreams one after another. It was as if she sailed a beautiful river and saw one wonderful farm after another, with houses all white and slate roofs and gilded lightning rods and cattle lolling in the shade of red barns. Anton would like a farm in this country. He said so. She felt the money in her grouch bag.

The dream intoxicated her.

Circus Parade

Then a voice said, "Hello, Lila, you sleepin'?"

"Oh no, Anton. I was chust dreamin'. Come on in an' siddown. Here—over here—dot's fine."

Anton smiled confidently while Lila wiped her forehead with an insufficient square of lace.

"My ain't it warm tonight?" she asked.

"It sure is," replied Anton while actually wondering why she had no oil heater in her tent.

He moved closer to her. "Lila, you do like me, don't you—you like me a lot, don't you, dear—you're my real friend, hain't you, dear?"

She rubbed her heavy hands together.

"Oh more so than a friend do I like you, Anton—much more so than a friend—much more so—I wonder kin you know how much more so, Anton."

"Yes, I know. That's fine, dear," returned Anton, looking about at the tent's tawdry disarray.

"You know the season's closing soon, don't you, Lila?"

"Dot's right," assented Lila, moving closer to Anton.

"Well you see, Lila—I'm broke—and I wondered——"

"Oh never mind dot, Anton. I'm so much more than a friend, never don't mind dot. I have got plenty for both."

[136]

The Strong Woman

"That's fine of you, Lila—you're a peach—you'll make a wonderful wife. You sure got it on Marie five ways from Sunday. I'm offa her the more I see of you, little one." A pause.

"You know, Lila," he resumed, "I get tired of the show business, as I told you before. I'd like to settle down, wouldn't you? I gotta letter today from a buddy. He's got the finest little piece of land with a lake on it."

"Yah, yahh. Go on, go on," said Lila.

"Well a fellow could get it for three thousand, and he could raise everything on it. Why they say the wild geese come there by the thousands. And you can sell 'em for a dollar apiece.

"It's a trick lake, Lila. The geese light on it in the winter and it freezes over every night. Then all you have to do is to wait till morning and go out in a boat and load it with geese. You can catch forty thousand geese every winter that way. He told me about it because he's got a gold mine near Pittsburgh and ain't got time to work the farm any more. Says he's tired of draggin' geese offen the lake."

"Is dot so? How good dot is," smiled Lila.

"I'll say it's good, Lila. The house is on a big hill an' you can see through the trees for miles and

Circus Parade

miles. Gosh, I never had such a good time. I sure wish I could buy the place, but then I ain't got no money. You know I got hurt last year. Making the last mount, my foot slipped offa Benito's shoulder an' I spilled—cracked three ribs. It's kep' me broke ever since."

"Why you poor boy," said Lila, "poor boy. And yust to think you must work now." She stroked his hair. "Why diden' you ask for more money?"

"Well it is pretty tough, Lila, but, you know, I'm all man I am. I never whimper. I got an old mother an' I'm good to her. She always says to me, she says, 'A boy who'll be good to his old mother'll be good to any other woman,' an' I always pet her an' say, 'Shut up, ma, you old jollier.' Course away down deep I admire women. If it wasn't for women, how'd any of us get here?"

There never was such a light in Lila's eyes before.

"You good, good boy," she said, holding his head against her ample bosom, large enough for the miseries of the world. "Such a good boy—an' dot little lake dat the geese come to—poor geese. We'll let your mudder stay wit' us too. An' we won't hurt the geese."

"You know, Lila, I'm learnin' to think a lot o'

The Strong Woman

you. You're a mighty fine woman. You got a heart in you bigger'n all outdoors. I ain't never seen a woman like you, I ain't."

Anton laid his arm on her immense shoulder. Her eyes closed. Little lines of joy ran around them.

"Oh, I am so happy," she exclaimed, holding Anton to her as gentle as a mother holds a babe.

"I just knew—I just knew. I been a good girl all the time, Anton. Some man I knew would care for good girl. Oh, Anton, how good, how nice, how sweet you are." She sobbed, her tremendous bosom moving.

"But, Lila, any man must care for you. How capable you are and how strong."

"Oh, Anton, I do be strong, but you don't know how hard it be before you come. So lonesome, all the time I sit an' read an' want my man too, an' my little house an' my lake an' my geese an' odder tings like odder women. An' here all time I leeft men an' cows an' tings. Oh, I'm so *hapee*, so *hapee*." She clapped her hands together. Anton jumped at the noise.

"I leeft sometimes an' my shoulders they hurt, an' nobody t'inks dot I ever be seeck. But oh, Anton, I do be sometime so seeck, I cannot see all du people who gawk at me a liftin' farmers."

Circus Parade

"That's a tough life, dearie, but you know it won't last forever. There's happier days ahead now." He put his arms partly about her. "Wonderful woman," he crooned, "just like a little girl." There was a joyful pause for Lila.

"Can you cook, girlie?" asked Anton.

"Oh yes, yes, Anton, I can cook everyt'ing an' can make lager be-er unt schmearkase—unt—unt——"

"Well, well that'll be fine. I'll tell you, Lila, what do you say we buy that little farm I told you about? I can wire my friend fifteen hundred if you say so. Then we can get married the last day of the circus here. And by that time my friend'll have everything fixed for us, and we can go right there. It ain't far to New York State from here. It's only eleven now, an' I can git down and wire the money before twelve."

"Oh dot'll be fine, Anton. Here, I give two thousand to you." She took her grouch bage from her neck and handed the money to him. "Blessy boy, so good, so kind, so much more'n a friend. I love you —so much—much more. You breeng me happeeness."

Anton's hands shook as he took the twenty hundred dollar bills.

The Strong Woman

"Don't shake, Anton Boy, I'm happier'n you," Lila said as she rose and walked with him to the tent door.

"I'll be back in an hour. It may take a little longer, but don't worry, girlie, I'll be here sure." Anton smiled as he kissed her cheek.

She was too happy to read for the next hour. . . .

*   *   *

In three mornings they found her in crumpled finery. A little blue bottle was clenched in her right hand. Many paper-backed novels were piled near her trunk. It was packed as if for a long journey.

IX: "With Folded Hands Forever"

IX: "With Folded Hands For-ever"

THE Strong Woman's death had a gloomy effect upon me. Slug Finnerty and Cameron had discovered her. A mark was seen on her throat, as though the string which held her grouch bag had been torn from it. Money, jewelry, finery, everything of possible value had disappeared. We always felt that Cameron and Finnerty had robbed her.

"They'd of skinned her if they could, the measly crooks!" sneered Jock. "Talk about fallin' among thieves."

The coroner was called, and signed the death certificate. There was no money with which to bury her.

"It's a lucky shot for me," said Silver Moon Dugan, "I owed her fifty bucks I won't have to pay. She was a funny dame."

The Moss-Haired Girl said to me after the coroner had gone, "It sure is awful to die in Arkansas with this circus, but then she's just as well off. She

[145]

was just in wrong, that's all." She walked with me to where the Baby Buzzard sat in front of the musicians' tent.

"Well, she's gone," said the Baby Buzzard as we approached.

"Yes," was Alice's answer.

"It's a hard loss for Bob. She drew a lot of money each week."

"Yes, it's *too bad* for Bob. *Poor Bob*, he does have the *hardest time*," smiled Alice.

"Yes indeed he do," responded the Baby Buzzard, missing the Moss-Haired Girl's tone of mockery.

"But she has to be buried, you know," continued the Moss-Haired Girl. "There's too much of her to keep above ground. We'd better take up a collection for her. I'll start it with twenty dollars." Just then Cameron appeared. "What will you give?" Alice asked him.

"Well, I think five dollars each among twenty of us will be enough. After all, we can't get a coffin big enough in the town, and it don't matter anyhow. I've got two of the boys makin' a big box and linin' it wit' canvas. The coffins fall apart after three days in the grave anyhow. Them undertakers

"With Folded Hands Forever"

are the original highway robbers." And Cameron fingered his Elk tooth charm.

The Baby Buzzard disappeared and returned with her glassful of half dollars. She counted ten of the coins and handed them to Alice, who turned them over to Cameron.

"These'll pay her way through purgatory, or start her soul rollin'. That's more'n she'd do for me if I croaked. People 'at croak 'emselves should bury 'emselves. Them's my ways of lookin' at it. I ain't never seen a man yet I'd bump myself off for. You can't do 'em no good when you're dead," half soliloquized the Baby Buzzard.

"May be not," returned the Moss-Haired Girl, looking from Cameron to the Baby Buzzard, "but we can at least shut our mouths and let her rest in peace. Somebody's stole everything she had. Even her silk underwear's gone. And who in the dickens with this circus can wear that?"

"Maybe Goosey stole it to put on the elephants," sneered the old lady.

"Maybe so, but the elephants wouldn't wear it if they knew it was stolen. They're above that."

"Well, well," and Cameron now became reverent, "it's all beyond our power." He pointed heaven-

[147]

ward. "He who is above us has called her home."

"He may have called her, but He didn't send her carfare. He probably thought she could bum her way," dryly commented the Baby Buzzard.

"That is not for us to judge," replied Cameron solemnly, "for who are we to question the Great Taskmaster's laws? It is best that we bury her before parade so as not to disturb the even tenor of our ways. I will say a few words and have the band play and sing a few songs. And then we shall take her to the graveyard in one of the elephant's cages. Buddy Conroy is there now makin' arrangements. The wagon with the cage can follow along with the parade, and no one will be the wiser."

The Strong Woman was placed in a square pine canvas-covered box with her blonde head resting on a huge red pillow trimmed in green. Her heavy hands were folded. Her mouth was puckered in a half smile which helped to conceal the cyanide scar at the edge of her lower lip. Her head was buried in the pillow. Her large breasts rose high above everything.

Fourteen men lifted the box.

Cameron's showman instinct prevailed at the last. The calliope was called into service. A man stood upon its platform and played as weird a tune as was

"With Folded Hands Forever"

ever concocted by the most fantastic human brain.

It seemed to my boyish mind to have been blended with wild wails and screeching laughter. It was followed by:

> *I had a dream the other night,*
> *Floating on the River of Sin,*
> *I peeped inside of Jordan bright,*
> *Floating on the River of Sin,*
> *And another place I seen inside,*
> *Floating on the River of Sin.*
> *A place where the devil does reside,*
> *Floating on the River of Sin.*

Freaks and thieves, trailers and clown acrobats and stake-drivers gathered in front of the Strong Woman's tent.

"Come on now, men, we'll make it snappy," said Slug Finnerty. "Join in the song with the calliope."

He waved his hands.

> *I seen a band of spirits bright,*
> *Floating on the River of Sin,*
> *Holding church by candle light,*
> *Floating on the River of Sin.*
> *A great big chariot passing by,*

Circus Parade

Floating on the River of Sin,
Come so close they had to fly,
Floating on the River of Sin.

The crude heavy voices were drowned out by the wail of the calliope.

They drove the chariot down below,
A spirit fell down and hurt his toe,
Floating on the River of Sin.
Then singin' and shoutin' way out loud,
Floating on the River of Sin.
They took her to heaven in a great big cloud,
Floating on the River of Sin.

When the song had died away Silver Moon Dugan, the Boss canvasman, commented.

"Gee, if she ever falls outta heaven there'll be a splash." A few roustabouts laughed. Then Cameron stood before us on a pine box.

"Fellow travelers with Cameron's World's Greatest Combined Shows," he began, and paused—"it is my sad duty to say a few words here. I wish it understood that I come to bury Cæsar, not to praise her. She is beyond us now, stripped of everything before God, who takes care of the weary and the

"With Folded Hands Forever"

worn and calls the wandering lady here home.

"We talk of worldly splendor, yet Solomon in all his gorgeous glory was not arrayed as one of these. She who now lies here before us once held our little world in awe. Now none of us are too procrastinatin' an' poor to show our irreverence, and she recks not at all of it. It is not ours to judge, for we are ever in the Great Taskmaster's eye, and if he should ever blink it ever so slightly we would crumble like the atomic mountains that rise outta the sea.

"Ours is but a little stay here, full of sound and fury, and, if you will pardon the blasphemy, signifying not a hell of a lot.

"It all reminds me of that well-known poem made immortal by Browning, than whom there was no more profound student of the human heart:

> *There is so much good in the best of us,*
> *And so much bad in the rest of us,*
> *That it little behooves the best of us*
> *To talk about the rest of us.*

"Those lines to me have always been a welcoming tocsin. When tired, when weary with the troubles of Cameron's World's Greatest Combined Shows, I

Circus Parade

often retire to my humble car and solicitate upon them. Feeling the full majesty of them, I have naught but love and understanding for those members of my circus who would fain be ungrateful.

"For are we not the same that our fathers have been? Do we not see the same sights and view the same sun and run in the same blood where our fathers have run?

"A great object-lesson can be received from this. As I have said in preceding, we are ever in our Great Taskmaster's eye. He who rolls the mountains is watching over us.

"God is ever on the side of justice, or as General Robert E. Lee so well said, God marches at the head of the heaviest battalions; and those battalions are imposed of justice and mercy and undying truth."

Cameron took a large red and white kerchief from his pocket. He unfolded it deliberately, then wiped his forehead and eyes, cleared his throat and resumed:

"We have labored in the vineyard with our sleeping friend here—and that reminds me that she is not dead, but sleepeth." Cameron looked at his audience as one will who feels he has uttered a profound truth. He wiped his eyes again. When he removed

[152]

"With Folded Hands Forever"

the kerchief they suddenly filled with tears. His whole manner changed. "Oh it stabs my heart, this grief before me. He who has loved and has run away may live to love some other day. But what about the victim of this dastardly attempt at liason? I adjure you . . ." His frame shook, his kerchief rubbed wet eyes. The audience looked bored with piety. Cameron's right hand, holding the kerchief, rose high in the air. He stood on tiptoe. "But friends, do not despair. In that vast circus ground in the other world we shall meet the lady who lies here with folded hands forever."

The crowd dispersed. The Strong Woman was placed in the elephant cage while the calliope played:

> *Room enough, room enough,*
> *Room enough in heaven for us all—*
> *Oh don't stay away.*

It then shifted:

> *At the cross, at the cross,*
> *Where I first saw light,*
> *And the burden of my heart rolled away,*
> *Rolled away—*

Circus Parade

It was there by faith
I received my sight,
And now I am happy all the day—
All the day.

The ringmaster's whistle blew. Wagons began to move. The Strong Woman started on her last parade.

X: Tiger and Lion Fight

X: Tiger and Lion Fight

A S the season became older the hatred toward Cameron grew sharper. Men of every description had come and gone since I had joined the circus in Louisiana. My salary was increased to seven dollars a week and board. I earned about the same amount running errands for the Baby Buzzard, the Moss-Haired Girl, and Finnerty and Jack. The Baby Buzzard gave me four half-dollars each week.

For many days I thought of the Strong Woman. I linked her up with the Lion Tamer and recalled the expression I often saw on her face as he passed her on the lot walking, graceful like a panther. Death again haunted me as in my childhood. These two—one buried in Louisiana, the other in Arkansas—did they know what we were doing? I wondered who jerked the Strong Woman's grouch bag from about her throat, and if Anton would ever hear of her death.

The old trailer, who had written the verses when the Lion Tamer died, was no longer with us. He had refused to follow the circus through Arkansas. We

Circus Parade

had played three days in Little Rock. I last saw him in a saloon near the Iron Mountain railroad. He had been drunk three days and was just trying to sober up. Jock and I had stepped in for a drink. He sat, looking disconsolate, with his elbows on a beer-stained table.

As we walked over to him, he said, "Won't you buy me a drink, boys? My nerves are all gone, my head aches awful an' my mouth feels like a Chinese family's just moved out."

The words pleased Jock and he laughed heartily. Loungers in the saloon turned to look at us.

"You old reprobate, that's worth a half pint." Jock placed the coin on the bar. The bartender held a bottle and asked sharply, "What do you want, rye or bourbon?"

"I don't give a damn," the old man answered impatiently, grabbing at the bottle, removing the cork and placing it to his mouth. We watched the old man drink it like water. Jock gave him a quarter with, "Ain't you trailin' us any more?"

"Not no more, no siree. I don't trail no circus in Arkansas. The God damn rubes down there ain't begun to be civilized. Whenever I hit Little Rock I jist turn round and go back no matter where I'm headin'."

Tiger and Lion Fight

As we left, the old trailer handed us each a poem printed on yellow paper.

"It's a little thing I wrote the other day. I like it too. It's all about booze."

Jock crunched the paper in his hand. I looked at my copy as we walked toward the circus lot.

It was Edgar Allan Poe's "Raven." The first line had been changed from

Once upon a midnight dreary

to

One summer morning bright and cheery,
While I pondered weak and weary . . .

The poem was called "A Drunkard's Fate," and was signed by the old trailer.

We encountered a rainy week in the heart of Arkansas. Our nerves, for the most part, worn threadbare from long contact with one another, now grew more taut as one dreary day followed another down the wet road of time. Even the animals became moody and sulky. Jock, full of morphine, swore terribly at the horses, until his "habit" had worn off.

As our bunks were full of vermin, or "crummy" in the vernacular of the circus, we slept in the circus

Circus Parade

wagons and other places on warm nights. Now that the air was chilled with rain we were forced to our vermin-infested bunks. My own fortunes were to change later when Whiteface became a clown. He was allowed a little tent to himself. I shared it with him.

Mike Anderson, who had succeeded Denna Wyoming as lion tamer, took us one day in a body before Cameron. He met us affably, even benignantly, with, "Well, boys."

"We're tired of floppin' in the lousy bunks, Mr. Cameron," Mike said suddenly.

"Why men," Cameron returned quickly, "this is surprising. Lice and rubes are part of a circus."

"Maybe so, but I don't want either of 'em in my bunk," sneered Anderson.

Just then the Baby Buzzard approached.

"I suppose you want me an' the other women to clean 'em for you," she snapped.

"Naw we don't. We want 'em all burned up an' new ones put in."

The adroit Cameron soon placated the feelings of all his callers but Anderson. He stood sullenly by while Cameron said with soft voice, "You know how it is, men, keeping a circus clean is a hard job."

"Ringlin's do it," put in Anderson.

[160]

Tiger and Lion Fight

"But look at the many localities they have; they got everything convenient. Next year, if this rain stops, I'll have a much finer circus an' it'll be like a little home for all of us."

As we walked away Anderson confided to me, "Tomorrow's pay-day. I think I'll blow the outfit."

The next day Cameron explained to all who would listen the hardships of a circus owner's life, as he reluctantly paid us.

Anderson was paid in full. He also borrowed twenty dollars from Cameron, who wished to keep him in good humor. Men who could handle animals of the cat tribe were scarce so late in the season.

Cameron had offered Jock more wages to take charge of the "Big Cats" than he was receiving for taking care of the horses. Knowing always the condition of his nerves, he refused.

Bad Bill had been separated from the other lions on account of the growing fierceness of his disposition. Anderson had placed him in a cage next to Ben Royal, a Bengal tiger.

I had often speculated on whether or not Ben Royal could whip Bad Bill. He was at least forty or fifty pounds lighter. I had remembered reading in a history of Rome, as a child, that five lions had always been sent into the arena against four tigers.

[161]

Circus Parade

That seemed proof to me that the tiger was the lion's master. I had once talked about it to Denna Wyoming. "Bad Bill," said he, "can lick anything that walks or swims in the world." Anderson, then the chief assistant trainer laughed out loud when I told him about it.

"Ben Royal kin tear Bill's heart out in three minutes," was his comment. The idea of a fight between Bad Bill and Ben Royal afterward fascinated Anderson. He would often refer to it. And once, after I had talked to him about the ancient combats in Rome, "That'd be a battle, huh! We oughta git old Cameron to stage one for us."

It was Bad Bill whom Denna Wyoming had feared most of all. Anderson had shared his fear. Jock also hated and feared him. Though he was not directly responsible for Denna's death, both men distrusted him as Wyoming had done. Jock had often called Bad Bill a traitor. He seemed to hold it against him that Wyoming had once saved his life with huge mustard plasers. In some way he resented the fact that the dumb king of beasts was ungrateful. That day Anderson and Jock talked a long time.

All night the rain fell drearily and, in spite of the parafin, soaked the tents. The next morning, before

[162]

Tiger and Lion Fight

breakfast, an alarm sounded over our canvas world. Anderson was nowhere to be found. The rope which held the partition which separated Ben Royal and Bad Bill had been cut. Many of us had heard a lion roar in the night but had paid no further attention. Bad Bill was found, his throat torn, his stomach ripped open, and part of his carcass eaten. Ben Royal, with bloody jaws, dozed near him.

"Can you beat it?" laughed Jock to me. "Anderson sure as hell turned Ben loose on Bill. The son of a gun wanted to turn him loose on Cameron."

Cameron was grief-stricken. "Two thousand dollars gone to hell," was his dismal moan for some days.

The tiger was afterward billed as "Ben, the Lion Killer." A stirring tale of his combat was written and placed on his cage. Anderson was never found again.

"Anderson knew Ben 'ud kill Bill," Goosey afterward told me. "The lion has everything buffaloed but the tiger. When I was wit' Wallace I seen a tiger kill two lions quicker'n you could say 'have a drink.'

"The lions seen the tiger comin' an' roared loud as thunder but it gave a lunge wit' its mouth wide open and caught the one lion right under the throat an' before it got thru' gurglin' it copped the other

Circus Parade

lion. They had to turn a big hose on him to git him outta the cage. He sure went snarlin'!"

Goosey never tired of talking about animals.

"I seen a half lion and half tiger once," he told me. "But they coulden go no further wit' it; they can't have little ones; they either come straight lions or straight tigers the second time.

"A tiger kin outjump a lion too. I seen 'em jump over sixty feet. All's a lion kin do is 'bout forty-five. But they don't like to jump, it hurts their feet. They're jist as careful as a housecat about their paws."

Goosey was placed in charge of the "big cats" until another trainer could be found.

Cameron never forgot the twenty dollars he had advanced Anderson. He used it as an excuse when asked for money during the remainder of the season.

XI: A Day's Vacation

XI: A Day's Vacation

FOR three more days it rained. Our very lives were soggy. The last town had been a bloomer. Not enough money had been taken in at the gate to pay expenses. Cameron was sad. And still it rained. We hoped, the derelicts of circus life, that by the grace of God and the winds of chance we would again see the sun.

The performers were able to travel in some comfort. But the canvasmen, hostlers and stake-drivers, were not so fortunate. We protected ourselves from the maddening rain by crawling under pieces of side-wall canvas atop the wagons. In spite of the rain, we tried to sleep.

The cars lurched noisily from one tie to another through the rainy night. There were no clouds; just the raindrops stabbing through the heavy steel atmosphere.

Once in the pathos of disgust I started to sing, "I wish I was in Dixie, Hurray! Hurray!"

"Shut up, you dog, or we'll lynch you for cruelty

Circus Parade

to animals," the jockey yelled above the creaking of the wagons.

I hummed "Rock of Ages" and tried to doze again.

Still a boy, my heart beat lighter then. All life was a pageant where now it is a slow parade.

But I did have one concern. Burrowed under the canvas not ten feet from me was an immense pounder of stakes in whose head several screws had suddenly loosened. It was shaped like a lead bullet that hit a granite wall. Over it was blonde clipped hair that looked like stubs of withered grass.

His nose had been smashed to the left. Each eyeball was permanently fixed in the left corner of his eye. He could not look to the right without turning half way round. But his appearance did not bother me. I had always been certain from the day he joined the show that he was an escaped lunatic, though it was too personal a question to discuss with him.

I had no reverence, and the blonde giant was a religious fanatic. He talked loud and long about Sodom and Gomorrah, as though he felt I was an outlaw from those unhappy places. I had once innocently said to him, "I wonder who makes God's raincoats. You know he's a big guy and I'll bet it takes all the canvas in a Barnum tent just to pad his shoulders. He should give a God damn about it

[168]

A Day's Vacation

rainin' on us guys." I had made the remark merely as a philosophical speculation, being very young. But the blonde gentleman was a Christian and became my mortal enemy.

Some days before I had picked up a little dog, the majority of whose ancestors had been Fox terriers. He was all white, save for the end of his stubby tail, which was black. I met him on the circus lot. He was so joyful and carefree, and so glad to see me that I held him in my arms a long time.

I called him Jeremiah. The daintiest of women have since tripped in and out of my life, but little stub-tailed Jeremiah remains my first remembered love.

We trekked with the circus together with no subtleties, and no explanations, our hearts laid bare to one another. I was not a tramp circus kid to Jeremiah, but a traveling gentleman who loved dogs. I write this in explanation of my love for him. It has bulked large through the years.

Jeremiah now slept under the canvas with me. The huge blonde man thought I was making fun of religion whenever I called to the dog. Just the day before he had kicked at Jeremiah, and missed him. I saw the act and tangled with the stake-driver. Jeremiah, in his haste to help me, started to bite,

Circus Parade

but the little rascal got the wrong leg. Silver Moon Dugan pulled me away from the big blonde.

I could now hear the man moving uneasily under the canvas. I had, like many others, tried to sleep in the bunks. The vermin had routed us all. Now it was anywhere out of the wet.

I would doze fitfully, alert for defense if the blonde should want to rid a sinful world of my presence. Jeremiah seemed to sense my uneasiness, and kept burying his nose under my armpit.

In this manner we jolted on through the rain-drenched night.

We reached a muddy suburb of Atlanta with early dawn. When we unloaded the circus, Jock was compelled to go into Atlanta for more horses to pull us.

Roxie, the best elephant with the show, had worn her forehead raw, pushing out wagons bogged in the mud. Jumpy had made a pad for it out of an old army blanket and a quilt. The heavy poultices dripped with water which ran down her trunk. She was in an evil mood. She clomped through the mud swinging her trunk madly.

After much trouble we were on our way to the circus grounds. A wind came up and sizzed through the rain. Lanterns hung on each wagon. The wind made them bob up and down as if they floated on

[170]

A Day's Vacation

water. Lanterns were also attached to the neck yoke of the lead horses. From the distance we must have resembled an immense glowworm crawling through space.

Jock worked horses and men with driving energy. An eight-horse team traveled up and down by the side of the road, with a heavy snake chain dragging behind. This was used in pulling wagons out of the mud.

We reached Atlanta at daylight. Within an hour the sun shone over the city. It pierced red through the hazy weather.

On our way to the circus grounds I noticed that the Southern Carnival Company was in Atlanta.

The blonde stake-driver threw a spasm in the cook tent. His hands and knees went together, his eyes stared more rigidly to the left, he jumped high in the air, and fell on the ground as stiff as an iron bar.

We laid him out on a water-soaked bunk.

Silver Moon Dugan, the boss canvasman, mumbled, "A hell of a time to throw a fit, jist when the tent's goin' up." He was short of men as usual. I helped put up the tent.

With the hope of breaking the monotony by attending the carnival, I asked Jock if I might not

Circus Parade

play sick that day and join him after the night performance.

He said, "Sure, go ahead. It's too wet to parade anyhow. I'll fix it up."

Jock gave me a silver dollar. I took Jeremiah with me.

We walked slowly along until we came to a small butcher shop where I bought some meat for the dog. I was glad to be away from the blonde man, and Jeremiah would look up at me as if he were trying to express the same emotion. With no immediate worry save that of obtaining food, I loitered about Atlanta with Jeremiah until mid-afternoon.

My mind was on the Southern Carnival Company. All such aggregations worked a shell game through the South. I had learned many things from Slug Finnerty's crew. Accordingly I sauntered through one alley after another with Jeremiah in the hope of finding rubber out of which to fashion a pea.

After a long search I came upon an old-fashioned clothes-wringer. As no one was about I soon removed one of the rubber rollers and carved a chunk from it. After much shaping and polishing I made it resemble a pea turned dark from handling. When finished, I threw the rest of the roller on the ground. Jeremiah immediately picked it up and started carrying it

A Day's Vacation

with him. I bade him drop the possible circumstantial evidence and inquired my way toward the carnival.

Everything was in full blast when I arrived with Jeremiah and hunted up the shell game. A crowd had gathered.

I was attracted by the man who ran it. He stood perspiring under the hot sun. I leaned down and talked to Jeremiah, pointing to the ground at my feet, with the hope of making him understand I wanted him to stay close to me. He remained so close that I could touch him with my foot at any time. The operator of the shell game was jubilant.

"Here you are, folks. If you guess right, you win. That's all life is, folks, just a guess, folks—a question of guessing right. Three simple shells—under which shell is the pea, folks?" he kept saying as he rubbed his hands together.

He was shaved close. His jaw was steely blue with a streak of red across it, as if a razor had made a furrow that healed over, leaving a dent in the middle. The scar seemed to open and close as he talked, as though contradicting what his lips were saying. I looked about to spot the shillabers, his accomplices. There were several within a dozen feet of him.

Circus Parade

All about them were vari-colored rustics. The whites were burned red by the sun and the blacks could no blacker be. The latter were dressed in fantastic colors, like barbaric children from another world.

Assuming as much innocence as possible, I looked about in a scared manner. I needed someone to furnish the money. A young Negro stood close to me. The eyes of a born gambler danced in his head. Suddenly I heard the man with the scar across his jaw talk out of the corner of his mouth to a shillaber standing behind me, "Ushpay the pumchay oserclay." People in a canvas and semi-gypsy world have a language of their own. They shift a word about and always put "ay" at the end of it. In this manner they can carry on a conversation that no one else can understand. The sentence translated was "Push the chump up closer." There was a sudden movement from behind. I looked more scared than ever, as I talked to the young Negro near me.

Being shoved closer, I looked at the swiftly moving hands of the man with the scar on his jaw. They were long and well kept, except for the nail on the little finger of his right hand. It extended about half an inch.

His shirt sleeves were rolled above his black al-

[174]

A Day's Vacation

paca coat. Money of all denominations lay near his left hand. He handled it with indifference. "Just a mere guess, folks, a mere guess, that's all." He looked at me benevolently. I leaned down and patted Jeremiah who huddled between my legs for protection.

"You merely guess, folks, under which of the three shells the little black pea is hidden. If you guess right, I pay. Nothing intricate at all."

I watched him closely. He pretended to hide the pea awkwardly. Sometimes it even held up one side of the shell under which it was supposed to be hidden. He would give the shell a little push as if he had just discovered his error.

The play was slow at first. The operator offered ten to five, then twenty to a hundred and so on, alternating, "Come, gentlemen, locate the pea," he would say as he counted out the money. "Two dollars to one. But why not win more? Your money never grows in your pants pockets."

A large Negro laid down five dollars. His smile was forced and the look in his eye was too quick. I knew he was a shillaber. He turned a shell. The pea was not under it.

"Even money on the other two shells," declared the man. "I'll try it once for five," volunteered a

Circus Parade

young white shillaber who were a derby. He laid the five dollar bill down and flipped a shell over. There lay the pea. The man with the scar laughed as he paid out ten dollars.

"That's the way it goes, gentlemen. Lay down five and pick up ten. One man's loss is another man's gain. Try it once more there, colored boy," to the first player. He shifted the shells and the pea.

"I'll try it once moah if you all let my frien' heah pick it foh me," he suggested, at the same time pushing a chocolate-colored brother in front of him.

"I don't care who picks it, gentlemen, as long as you gamble fair and square," said the man.

The big colored fellow laid down another five dollar bill and turned to the other. "You go on an' pick it foh me. You looks lucky to me, boy." The latter grinned proudly and looked closely at the shells.

Several other Negroes told their comrade which shell the pea was under. The operator seemed engrossed in other matters as the Negro raised the shell and disclosed the pea. He then counted out the winnings and began to hand them to the little chocolate-colored man. The big Negro pointed out the operator's mistake and claimed the money.

[176]

A Day's Vacation

"My mistake, gentleman, my mistake," laughed the operator.

The big Negro said, "But you'd all of paid him he won, huh?"

"Certainly, gentlemen, certainly, whoever wins. It's merely the love of the play that keeps me here. I enjoy it as much as you, folks. I could easily, gentlemen, follow any other calling, but here is my life work, gentlemen, just the joy of taking a chance. A gambler at heart, gentlemen, a square shooter, a fair deal, gentlemen, and no favors. I paid one man five hundred last week. The turn of a shell, gentlemen, the turn of a simple shell, and a fortune underneath. The wealth of Minus, gentlemen, the wealth of Minus." He looked down at me. "If any other gentlemen had put their money down they would have won also."

The big colored shillaber began talking to the little man who had chosen for him. "Come, boy, you is lucky. I'll put five dollahs down and you puts five dollahs, then we both win. Come on, you otheh colohed boys." Several of them watched the studied clumsiness of the operator and pulled money out of purses with twist clasps—money earned under a burning sun.

Circus Parade

All the Negroes won, and doubled their bets. They won again and tripled. Then all lost.

I watched the operator's long fingernail sweep under the shell with the action of a scythe.

The colored youth next to me stood fascinated. He smiled confidently at me and I saw my chance.

"Listen, kid," I whispered to him, "I can beat that game. If you'll let me have ten to play, I'll get you twenty back. I know the riffle. We'll make a getaway and I'll meet you at the Salvation Army Hotel on Peachtree Street."

The big colored shillaber stood within five feet of us, so I whispered even lower. "Now if I play and win and yell, 'Go,' you've got to run like the devil away from Holy Water. Hear me?" The little Negro nodded, still smiling. The operator was saying, "As wealthy as Minus, gentlemen, as wealthy as Minus. Rockyfeller took a chance, everybody does. Which of the simple little shells is the pea under, gentlemen?"

A shillaber moved closer and placed ten dollars on the board. Then as luck would have it, he turned to the colored lad near me. "You pick it out for me this time, boy." The little fellow picked the middle shell—and—there was the pea.

He smiled more confidently at me.

A Day's Vacation

Another shillaber edged closer in friendly conversation with a sun-tanned yokel. "We'll show you where we're from. We'll pick out the right shell so often you'll think there's a pea under every darn one o' them," laughed the shillaber. The yokel laid down five dollars. The shillaber likewise. They won twice, then lost. The yokel had not hesitated, but he lost anyhow.

Another shillaber, with an Italian who looked like like a peddler, had some difficulty in getting close to the board. The operator said quietly—"Etlay ethay ogaday uckerslay up otay ethay cardbay." ("Let the dago sucker up to the board.") The way cleared for him at once.

I coaxed the young Negro to take a chance with me. At last he could stand the contagion of the play no longer. "Heah, white boy, you beats it if you all kin," he said, slipping me a ten dollar bill.

I touched Jeremiah with my foot, and pushed closer to the board, the Negro close to me.

"I'll bet ten, Mister, if you'll let me pick up the shell," I said innocently.

"Certainly, my boy, certainly, most assuredly. It merely saves me the labor of raising a simple shell. A straight and fair game, gentlemen, and you can raise any shell you wish. Merely a game of wits

[179]

Circus Parade

—guess work. He who guesses the best always wins in this and other games of life."

The Italian played ahead of me, also the suntanned yokel and others. Their bets ranged from one to ten dollars. Money went back and forth, the operator and his shillabers working fast. The shillabers asked questions, the operator talked swiftly and moved his hands nervously, thus keeping up the tension of the play.

He suddenly beamed at me. "If you still wish to pick your own shell up, my lad, that privilege is yours. You look like a brave gambler to me. You love the game as I do. So it's as you will, my boy, as you will. I believe in giving the young a chance. I was young once myself away back yonder," he chortled, placing a ten dollar bill between the first and second finger.

I laid the Negro's money on the board. The operator placed it between his fingers.

"The left shell," I said and raised it, handing him the pea I had carved in the alley. "Here it is, Mister. I win."

The operator looked startled. The scar on his face turned redder. His own pea was lodged in his long finger nail. Before he recovered I took the money

A Day's Vacation

from between his fingers and dodged low and was gone. Jeremiah was well ahead of me.

Looking back I saw the shillaber with the derby hat make a grab for my colored friend. I was soon lost in the crowd.

I hurried off the lot, the two ten-dollar bills in my hand. Realizing after some distance that no one was pursuing me, I thought of the tough spot in which I had left the lad who had loaned me the ten dollars.

"Oh well," I said to myself, "they can't do anything with him—maybe beat him up a little, that's all."

Then the thought came that they might do anything with a Negro in Atlanta.

So thinking I reached the Salvation Army Hotel on Peachtree Street.

Sitting in a pine chair was my colored friend.

"What all took you so long?" he asked, as I handed him a ten dollar bill.

His eyes went as big as eggs.

"Ge-mun-ently—this all I git?" he asked.

"Sure Boy, look at all the fun you had. You're lucky to get your ten back. I took all the chances. Suppose I hadn't showed up at all."

[181]

Circus Parade

"Gee, that's right," he said as I left with Jeremiah.

Jock smiled happily when I told him of the incident that night.

XII: Whiteface

XII: Whiteface

WITHIN three weeks Cameron's World's Greatest Combined Shows were so badly crippled on account of many desertions that the tents were raised in each town with great difficulty.

It is the custom with the wanderers of circus life to leave without notice, and often without money. Routes of other circuses are studied carefully in theatrical papers, so that many "jump the show" and join one in the same vicinity. They will often travel many hundreds of miles until they come to another circus appearing in the same city.

Barnum and Bailey's show was pitched for two days in Forth Worth, Texas, when we arrived. Four clowns, three musicians and one freak deserted in a body.

Whiteface was made a professional clown by accident.

Somewhere his ancestors must have made forgotten kings to laugh. He had been a stake-driver a short time before. There was a vast difference in

Circus Parade

swinging an eight-pound sledge and being a kinker. For the kinkers are the performers, the aristocrats of the circus world.

He was a natural clown. People laughed at everything he did. Where he came from no one knew. His features were aquiline. There were traces of Ethiopian, Caucasian and Indian in him. But in the South he was just another Negro.

There was an eagle-like expression about his mouth and nose. In his eyes was the meek look of a dove. His teeth were as even as little old-fashioned tombstones in a row. He gave one the impression of power gone to seed, of a ruined cannon rusting in the sun, or a condor with broken wings.

He was one of those people in the subterranean valley who somehow managed to grow and give something to a world that had no thought of him. Under the make-up of a clown his sombre expression left him. He pushed his magnificent yellow body around the ring in a tawdry fool's-parade. He did not walk, he shambled. Over his yellow face was the white paint of the clown. He was, in the language of the circus, a whiteface.

His start had not been conspicuous. Four clowns had deserted. Something had happened to another

[186]

performer. Whiteface had been helping tear down some aerial rigging, and to save a delay he had been asked to do a dance. All the kinkers or performers smiled as he consented. The audience would laugh at his attempt at dancing, and the aim was to somehow make the audience laugh.

Then something happened. The huge Negro, with the flat coarse shoes lined with brass in front, ambled on the platform like a man with no bones in his legs. He resembled an immense dummy held up with wire and allowed to sag in the middle. He looked about him helplessly. And then suddenly listened, as though for a firing-squad. Then held out his long left arm as if wanting to say a last word with the gunners. It was a stroke of uncouth genius. The terrific effect of it stunned even the ringmaster. There was that tremendous silence one feels only before an execution. Then the great heavy feet began to move.

They patted the wooden stage with the noise of a giant's hands being clapped together. The boneless body moved as if dancing to the roar of the elements. Then suddenly it stopped. He held out his hand for a second as before and ambled from the stage with the same tempo he had used in closing

Circus Parade

the dance. The applause went around the tent in mighty waves. He was forced back on the platform again.

There was a heavy silence. The heavy feet shook for a second and a heavier wave of appreciation rolled around the tent. Then the immense hand went out like a yellow talon outspread. It had the effect of a firing-squad again. In another second he had ambled from the platform.

Immediately he was prevailed upon to become a clown. He took the job with the same unconcern that he had taken that of stake-driving. He assembled his regalia and rehearsed by himself. He would inflict none of his three colors on the pure white strain of his brother clowns. But in justice to them, they were nearly all artists at heart and drew no color line.

Sufficient to himself as a stake-driver, he remained the same as a clown.

On the third night there wandered on the hippodrome track one of the weirdest of grotesqueries. The pathos and the laughter, the tragedy and the misery of life were stamped on its eagle face. And out of its eyes shone laughing pity.

People with the circus thought it was Jimmy Arkley putting on a new number. Jimmy was the boss clown and liked to do the unexpected. But Jimmy Arkley was standing on the sidelines himself. In his eyes were blended jealousy and admiration. For, bowing to right and left, was a master buffoon all unknowing.

He was using an old artifice to make his audience laugh, that of dignity being made ludicrous and still wrapping the remnants of dignity about itself. He was dressed as a king, with wide fatuous mouth and little shoe-button eyes. His crown was formed from a battered dish-pan and his sceptre was a brass curtain pole. A royal robe, trimmed with raw cotton, dragged on the ground behind him. The robe was so long that his scurvy pet alley-cat used it as a vehicle upon which to ride. Time after time the king would fall out of character long enough to chase the cat from the robe. But as soon as he continued his royal promenade the cat would get on the robe again. In his confusion the king would stumble over an imaginary obstacle.

After regaining his balance he was all dignity again. It was tragic to have so many unforeseen things happen just at the time he was showing himself to his subjects. But the more he suffered the more his subjects laughed.

When he had made his sad round of the hippo-

Circus Parade

drome track and the curtains of the back entrance hid him from view, he took the scurvy alley-cat in his arms and said:

"Well, Bookah, we done made 'um all laugh."

And Booker T. Washington licked the fatuous mouth of his master.

The audience was still chuckling over the king's exit. The manager hurried to find out who the new kinker was. The discovery that the king was none other than John Quincy Adams, the roustabout stake-driver, was a surprise. The manager told him to go ahead with the act, and gave him a raise of five dollars a week. This brought his salary up to fifteen dollars. He hugged the scurvy cat and said, "Heah, Bookah, take youh tongue outta my eye."

Jimmy Arkley of course was called in as the boss clown. He explained in detail to John Quincy Adams all the tricks which the dark gentleman with the scurvy cat knew by intuition.

As a stake-driver the name of John Quincy Adams meant nothing. As a clown it meant even less. There are no names like John Quincy Adams in the circus Almanac de Gotha. But as I've said before, somewhere his ancestors must have made forgotten kings to laugh. Whether it was during the period of the American Revolution I know not. As laughter is an

Whiteface

hysteria that defies analysis, being synonymous with religious fervor or patriotic outbursts, people laughed at John Quincy Adams without knowing why. Jimmy Arkley always sent him on when the audience was cold. It made no difference to John Quincy Adams. He always got the same laughter.

Even though Jimmy Arkley kept him in his place, life opened like a melon sliced for John Quincy Adams. He had found expression.

He was made to assist in the smaller clown numbers. He took the brunt of physical jokes perpetrated in the arena. He was always the clown upon whom the bucket of water was thrown. It was John Quincy Adams who was dragged by the trick runaway horse. It was his great yellow body that stopped the majority of the slapsticks.

He never complained.

Jimmy Arkley did not like him. But the sad-eyed clown liked all the world and could not see dislike in others. The huge bulk of John Quincy Adams was supersensitive to pain. Who would expect a Negro stake-driver to have acute sensibilities? Every time he winced under the blows of his brother buffoons the audience laughed the more. It was indeed remarkable the expression of pain he could focus on his white-painted face.

Circus Parade

His individuality survived it all. It was so marked that Jimmy Arkley was forced by the manager to allow him the center of the stage. He was even consulted about new numbers. At such times the great intuitive clown reverted to the stake-driver and became humble in the presence of whiter and lesser men.

But he never entered the pad-room, never dressed in the long tent with the other clowns. He still ate in the roustabout's section of the cook-house. His increase in salary was of benefit only to me and the scurvy cat. The latter was now heavy and dreamed for the most part nearly all of its nine lives away on John Quincy Adams' bunk. We three lived together in a small tent. It was away from the other tents. Whenever we moved to a new town John Quincy Adams would raise the tent alone.

He could neither read nor write. Once when I told him of a tragic paper-backed novel I was reading, he said:

"What all good dat do you, boy? You's alive ain't you? You doan have to read 'bout nothin'."

He spent his time playing solitaire, or manipulating new tricks with dice.

He could sing well. His voice was full of the tragedy of three races. He was fond of the Southern

folk songs, though he never quite got the words of
them correctly. A sense of drama, or an inarticulate
feeling for beauty made him accentuate some lines
and sing them over and over. When doing so he
would put out his immense hand as he had when
he first danced. I learned that it was a habit with him
when deeply moved. He would chant with a rolling
vibration, the wonderful quality of it choking me
with emotion and even making the cat stop licking
its scurvied scars and look up as the words poured
out, the chanter's body slouching low.

H–i–s fingers were l–o–n–g l–i–k–e c–ane in—the
   br–ake—
And he—had—no—eyes—foh—to see——

And then, as softly as dawn in the desert:

A few—more days—for—to tote de weary l–oa–d,
No mat–teh . . . t'w–ill nevah—be light——
A few moah—yeah–s till I—totteh daown de—
   road. . . .
D–en my old Kaintucky—home—goodnight——

His face at the end of such a verse was a mask
of concentrated agony. The heavy lips would quiver.
   I have often thought of him since, and of the

Circus Parade

scurvy cat we both loved. Three rovers of desolation, we had been joined together by the misery of inarticulate understanding. The cat was quite a personality. There were many places on his body upon which the fur would not grow. He spent hours shining these spots, like a battered old soldier eternally dressing his wounds.

Even when the clown took the cat in his arms and sang:

> *My masteh had a yaller gal,*
> *And she was from the Souf;*
> *Her hair it kinked so berry tight,*
> *She coulden' shut her mouf—*

the cat looked bored.

Success did not affect John Quincy Adams. Somewhere in his roving life there had been planted in his soul the futility of human vanity. So humble and self-effacing was he among the kinkers, that most of them forgot the master of pantomime in the person of the ex-stake-driver.

As the weather grew colder we trekked toward that strip of Florida which projects into the Gulf of Mexico.

It was a happy wandering along the Gulf. There

Whiteface

was a lazy indifference to life that we of the gypsy
clan loved. The brilliant sunshine was reflected everywhere. Even the shadows were diffused with
light. The air was balmy.

We played three days in some of the towns. That
allowed us to wander about a great deal. For the
longer a circus plays in a town the easier it becomes
for kinkers and flunkies. The work becomes a mere
matter of detail, like in a penitentiary or any other
institution.

So I often took long walks with John Quincy
Adams and the cat. Once in a while the clown was
touched with the wand of reminiscence. Booker T.
Washington, however, was always the same sad
fellow. Bright sunshine and green lapping waves
could not get his mind away from the patches that
made his hide look moth-eaten. Often, as John
Quincy and I looked out at the far green water upon
which white ships sailed, Booker T. Washington
would turn away as if scornful of our illusion of
beauty. He was an epic of boredom.

Only one thing marred the happiness of our
world. It was the year of a presidential election,
and owing to the uncertainty of how the pendulum
of politics would swing, the powers that be re-
trenched financially. Times became hard.

Circus Parade

As a consequence there was more friction between the colored and white races in the section through which we journeyed.

Many fights occurred.

But John Quincy Adams was not at all concerned by the animosities of differently colored men. It was not in his yellow hulk to inflict pain. He cringed, however, at each tale of physical violence he heard. Always there came into his face the look of concentrated agony. And once, when a Negro had been laid out with a rock, he said to me,

"What foh men 'buse each other?"

"I don't know, Quince," I replied. "There were probably some Irish in the gang."

He laughed, his grave-yard of teeth showing.

"Yeah, Red Boy, theah was some niggahs too, I'll bet."

"No, I don't think so, Quince," I said banteringly. "The Niggers and the Irish like each other. You know they both had to make a long fight for freedom."

John Quincy Adams was slouching low in the tent. He looked across at Booker T. Washington, who had just finished licking the patch above his paw.

"Did you heah that, Bookeh T.? Did you all heah

Whiteface

what the Red Boy says? He done read dat in one o'
dem books, Bookeh T. He doan know what we
know." His voice trailed off. . . . "Niggah an' de
Irish like each other." Then he turned toward
Booker T. Washington and me. "You done heah
that song, ain't you, Red Boy, the niggah sing?

I'm a goin' to put on my shoes and put on my coat,
An' am goin' to walk all oveh God's Heaben——

"Well, that ain't nevah so—now or no otheh
time." He laughed loudly.

"Heah's what happened. A big black niggah goes
prancin' into heaven an' all the streets was lined
wit' gold and silber lampposts an' big green an'
black pahrots a carryin' 'Merican flags in dere claws
kep' shoutin' out, 'Heah's de way, brotheh black
man,' an' dey leads 'em right up to de peahly gates,
an' right at de cohneh was a big chaih made outta
oysteh shells, an' de oystehs was a sittin' up in deah
shells a singin':

> *It's de land ob de free*
> *An' de home ob de slave,*
> *Sis-teh, sis-teh.*
> *The Lawd heals all youh wombs.*
> *Glor—ry, Glory, Glor—eee, glor—ee,*
> *The Lawd heals all youh wombs.*

Circus Parade

"De big niggah he goes a prancin' by, a washed all black in de blood ob de lamb, an' goes a slidin' up de corrydoor towahds de Great God Almighty who's a standin' theah waitin'. Then you should all hab seen dat niggah tuhn all reddah'n youh haih. A oysteh runs outta its shell and pinches his leg an' says, 'Heah you, niggah, you all is in de Irish section ob heaben. You kneels befoah youh God, you black bastahd.'

"God, he looks aroun' an' sees de oysteh an' says, 'Get youh back to youh shell. Oystehs should be seen and not heard.' Then God he tuhns to the niggah who's a kneelin' theah reddah'n a spanked baby, an' he says:

" 'What's youh all mean by this overdue familiahity? Doan you all know dis ain't youh heaven? Who tol' you come in heah, anyhow? I says to my pahrots not to leabe no niggahs in heah. Dis is Irish heaven, an' doan you know dey ain't no freedom wheah you sees birds carryin' the 'Merican flag? Dey carries dat for purtection w'en de win's git rough. Now you jist chase on outta heah, Black Boy, to niggah heaben. It's obeh deah back ob de slaughteh house.'

"The big niggah he walk away fasteh'n lightnin', an' God he done call out, 'Heah, you lazy oystehs,

Whiteface

scrub up dis place wheah de niggah's feet habe been. An' tell dem pahrots to let no moah niggahs in heah. Fuhst thing I know dese silber walks'll be all black.'

"Den de niggah he goes a singin' obeh towards de slaughteh house past wheah de dead oystehs is buried:

> *Jesus my awl to heaben has gone.*
> *Wheah is de stump I laid it on.*

"An' dat's how de niggah walked all obeh God's heaben. Dem niggah's is all de time kiddin' demselves."

The wind from the Gulf had turned colder. It moaned dismally about the tent as John Quincy Adams concluded his tale of the Negro in Irish Heaven. He had finished a hard day's playing to half-empty seats and was soon stretched out on the bunk with Booker T. Washington. Soon I could hear the cat purring and the uncouth pantomimist breathing heavily.

The night finally pushed its way into a drizzly morning. I went early to do my chores with the animals. They huddled forlornly together in the corner of their cages.

We loitered about until afternoon. A small crowd

Circus Parade

again turned out for the midday performance. A cold wind blew from the Gulf and all nerves were testy. Every person seemed to have a chip on his shoulder. The natives were hostile to the circus people.

"Somethin's goin' to happen in dis burg. I feels it in muh bones," was John Quincy Adams' comment at the supper table.

"Nope, you're all cold, Quince," I said. "Everything'll slip along all right and we'll breeze outta here tomorrow an' in two days we'll hit Miami. Then things'll break better."

"Maybe so, maybe so, but I done got a funny feelin'," was John Quincy's rejoinder.

That evening a colored man was said to have insulted a white woman. He had, intentionally, or otherwise, stepped ahead of her in the purchase of a ticket.

A white gentleman saw the act. He slammed the Negro in the jaw. The Negro, not knowing his place, slammed the white gentleman back. Another race riot started.

The Negroes connected with the circus disappeared as if by magic. Gangs of white men were looking for them everywhere.

When found, the Negro was sent running down

Whiteface

the road followed by rock salt and bacon rind from the guns of the whites. It was great fun until a colored man sent a real bullet through the arm of a white man and ducked under the circus tent.

The rules of the game had been broken. The white men now demanded blood. They surrounded the main tent like bush-beaters, closing in on a predatory animal. Carrying knives, guns and clubs, the avenging Southerners tramped through the tent.

I covered John Quincy Adams with a heavy blanket as the men came closer to our tent. With pounding heart I heard them talking as they searched.

"He ducked in here somewheres. We'll git him," one of them said.

After a seeming eternity of waiting a man pushed the flaps open and entered our tent. He was followed by five other men.

"You ain't got a nigger in here, have yu?" asked the leader.

"Nigger—hell no, what'ud a nigger be doin' in here?" I asked hotly.

Just then Booker T. Washington ran across the tent and burrowed under the blanket. With heartsick eyes I looked at him. The eyes of the five men followed.

[201]

Circus Parade

"You damn little liar," shouted the leader as he pushed me backward and rushed forward with the other men to the blanket. A shout went up.

"Here he is. We got him." Many more men entered the tent. A voice shouted, "That's him, that's the nigger that shot me."

Another man laughed. "Lookit him, tryin' to make up like a white man—paint smeared all oveh his mug."

The face of John Quincy Adams was full of pain. The gentlemen kicked and pushed him. He had the look of the doomed in his eyes as he looked about frantically. I thought of his abnormal dread of pain.

'He didn't do nothin', men. He's a white nigger," I pleaded.

"Get the hell outta here," snapped the leader. "We'll make him wish he was white. What was he hidin' for if he ain't the one?"

Several men held John Quincy Adams while two more swung vicious blows at his head. One man used a black-jack. John's head fell on his chest as though his neck had broken.

"I ain't nevah huht nothin'," he gasped weakly. A fist smashed against his mouth. Booker T. Wash-

[202]

Whiteface

ington rubbed against my leg. I picked him up and held him in the tensity of emotion.

Booted along, half walking and half dragged, his eyes covered with blood that flowed from the cuts in his head, John Quincy Adams was finally taken to a place where a fire was burning.

On the fire was a large square tin can into which chunks of tar were being thrown. Some of the tar fell into the flames and caused dense black smoke to curl around the heads of victim and persecutors.

"Les stake him to the fire an' burn him," yelled the man with the injured arm. "He'd a killed me dead if he could."

"Nope, les jist give him a nice overcoat o' hot tar," suggested another, "that'll hold him in his place for a while."

They tore his shirt from his body and threw it into the fire. Then his undershirt was torn into strips and stuck into the melting tar. I clung to Booker T. Washington.

There were moans as the tar was applied to the heaving body. The nauseating reek of burnt flesh and the odor of tar was everywhere.

The frenzy of the tormentors at last died down. They left the scene after kicking the prostrate form

[203]

Circus Parade

on the ground. The fire smouldered away in green-ish smoke as I approached the body of John Quincy Adams with Booker T. Washington in my arms. The white paint on his face was streaked with tar and blood.

His face was haggard, like that of a man crucified.

I knelt beside him while Booker T. Washington licked his face.

The wind blew in cold gusts from the Gulf.

But John Quincy Adams was forever unconscious of wind and weather.

XIII: An Elephant Gets Even

XIII: An Elephant Gets Even

THE term "goosey" is supposed to have originated with Southern Negroes. It covers a much larger meaning than the word "ticklish."

The victim is supersensitive to human touch. Once his malady is discovered by low class minds he finds little peace among them. He is continually being touched unexpectedly. His frantic actions at such times are the delight of his tormentors.

The elephant trainer's real name was William Jay Dickson. I learned it only by accident. His name with the circus members was always "Goosey."

Whenever Goosey was touched unexpectedly from behind, he would react with violence. If he happened to have a club in his hand he would strike the first object that stood in his way. If he had no club he would yell out loud the very thing of which he was thinking at the time. Once he was touched suddenly as the Moss-Haired Girl walked near him. He screamed.

"Lord, I'd like to love you." She turned about, saw his predicament and walked on smiling.

Circus Parade

Goosey would beg his tormentors not to tease him. No one paid him the slightest attention. It became a mania. If he heard a sound within ten feet of his rear, he would jump suddenly and either strike out or yell that which was in his mind.

Goosey had a surprising knowledge of animals gained from long practical experience. Elephants were his favorites. He had been around the world seven times, always in charge of elephants. He had spent a year in Africa with a man celebrated for his love of killing dumb brutes. Becoming disgusted with the wanton slaughter in the name of sport— it was really a tusk-hunting expedition—he deserted his employer in the Upper Congo. The experience haunted Goosey.

"When a elephant is shot it jist falls like the world comin' down. I jist couldn't stand it no more, for elephants don't harm nobody that don't harm them."

After Goosey deserted he made his way for miles through the jungle. The illiterate naturalist would watch a herd of elephants by the hour.

"I ain't never seen one of 'em lyin' down in my life. They don't never sleep. They kin smell you a mile off in the jungle an' the only way to fool 'em

An Elephant Gets Even

is to git aroun' so's the wind don't blow you in their direction.

"I've seen 'em dig big spuds up wit' their tusks. They nip 'em outta the ground like a farmer would wit' a hoe. An' they're right an' left handed wit' their tusks, jist like people. An' you can't fool 'em either. They allus know jist where they are, an' they know people better than people. They know how to take short cuts through the jungles in the dark an' they kin find them when travelin' as fast as a runnin' horse. You kin allus find 'em at the same place in the jungles every year. They're jist like a whale that way, they kin allus go back to where they was born in the ocean."

Goosey's chinless face smiled.

"I'll never forget the time I'd waited all winter to git a chance to take Big Jumbo from New York to Californie. I was broke flatter'n a nigger policeman's feet.

"I'd been with Jumbo the season afore an' got laid off at the end of it 'cause there wasn't enough coin to keep anybody but the main trainer. But he couldn't make the trip 'cause he was one o' them goofy married guys an' he has a skirt for a boss. He was no good animal trainer 'cause he let a woman run him, an' I says to myself, says I, 'There'll be

[209]

somethin' wrong wit' Jumbo if this guy takes care o' him long witout me.' "

Goosey hated all elephant trainers, but Jumbo's trainer at this time had his particular scorn. "He was a long tall drink o' water," went on Goosey, "an he believed in the honor o' women an' everything. He got sore once when I says to him, 'Who do you s'pose your wife steps aroun' wit' while you're chambermaidin' these elephants hither an' yon?'

"He looked at me tough an' says, 'You kin alluz tell when a guy was raised in the gutter by the questions he asks about the fair sex.'

" 'Maybe so,' I says, 'but you learn a heluva lotta things in the gutter that ain't in the books about women. When I was a kid I lived in a railroad division town. That's where you learn about women."

" 'What the hell's that got to do wit' it?' he says.

"Nothin',' I resounders, 'only when a railroader comes in off his run, he rings the front door bell an' beats it like hell aroun' to the kitchen jist in time to ketch the guy buttonin' his coat.'

" 'Again I asks you—what the hell's that got to do wit' it? You oughta be 'shamed o' yourself slanderin' the name o' womanhood that way.'

" 'I ain't a slanderin' 'em,' I says, 'I'm jista speakin' facks. A railroader's only away from his

[210]

An Elephant Gets Even

home a day or two, an' what in hell would happen if he was a elephant trainer an' gone all season?'

" 'For shame—for very shame,' he says, 'I'm from the South where women's held in rev'rence an' I thank God my mother was a good woman.'

" 'Well I hain't a sayin' nothin' against your mother, Boss, but they ain't none o' them any good. They're trickier'n a louse on a fiddler's head.'

"I don't think the Boss liked me after that. He knew that I knew he was a married goof an' we don't like nobody when they know we're goofs. So I think he was glad when he got a chance to ship me to Californie wit' Jumbo for the good o' his health.

"Well old Jumbo'd alluz been a fiend for milk. When he was a little baby not more'n four feet high an' not weighin' over a thousand pounds he'd chase a cow right down the aisle of a church and pump her dry. One time he chased a bull in New York State. Well he sure was disgusted.

"Well it come time for me to take Jumbo west. They had him all fixed up in a car at Yonkers; the crew was all ready, an', God, I was glad to be gittin' away from the snowballs to the warm sunshine.

"Well, sir, we hadn't any more'n started when Jumbo takes one breath and blows the side o' the car out, and lays right down an' dies."

Circus Parade

Goosey stopped at this memory of tragedy.

"I jist went nuts," he gasped. "Who the hell wanted a dead elephant in Californie?

"We cut him open an' there was eighty-eight cans o' condensed milk in him. He'd never even opened 'em—jist swallowed 'em whole.

"Well, sir, that cured me of havin' any guys that's nutty on women workin' on my elephant squad. I wouldn't care if Pope Pius the XV come to me for a job; he'd have to prove to me he wasn't married."

Laughter followed Goosey's words. He became more earnest, and rubbed the place where his chin should have been.

"An' you can't abuse an elephant either an' get away wit' it. They'll git you every time. I know when I first joined out I was jist a kid an' I worked under a guy up north. He'd brought a baby elephant up an' kep' whippin' it all the time. Indigo was the baby's name. An' Indigo was only afraid of one thing in the world an' that was his trainer, whose name was Bill Neely. He was a mean guy an' he wanted to make the elephant mean so's no one else could handle him. Then he could allus hold his job that way.

"By an' by Indigo got the rep of bein' a rogue elephant, a mean one. Neely used to like to show

[212]

An Elephant Gets Even

off wit' him. Every time Neely'd turn his back I'd see Indigo lookin' at him wit' his mean little eyes stuck out like billiard balls. Then when Neely'd turn aroun' an' look at him, Indigo'd begin to swing his trunk friendly like. An old boozefighter elephant man who used to work wit's us says to me one day, he says, 'Indigo'll kill him one o' these days jist as sure's Barnum was a crook. Now you watch.'

"We got so we begun to watch Neely jist like you would a guy they were goin' to hang. Then we got so we'd be nice to him 'cause we jist knew he wasn't goin' to live very long. But he was havin' a hell of a time. He'd carry the old bull hook an' prod Indigo every chance he got. The elephant'd wince an' stick its eyes out—then be nice agin.

"One time he was out showin' him off on the lot an' forgot hisself an' walked between Indigo an' the big cage where the hipplepotamus was. Then he prods him the last time while all of us was watchin'.

"Indigo gave a quick snort an' a shove an' Neely went smack against the wheel like a lotta mush. Indigo'd shoved him right through the spokes an' Neely never had time to say 'Boo.'

"There was more hell right then than you could shake a stick at. But Indigo didn't wait. He jist started runnin' hell bent for anything that was in

Circus Parade

his road. There was sure as hell some scramblin'. I damn near flew a gettin' outta his way 'cause the whole damn lot was his'n far's I was concerned. Who was me to interfere wit' his little fun?

"Indigo jist headed for the kitchen. He went right on through takin' the tent wit' him. 'Bout twenty gallons o' soup was on the stove. He never stopped for neither of them. He jist pushes the stove outta his way an' the soup flies all over him an' he smashes the big can, then he heads for the main tent an' goes right on through it like vinegar through a tin horn. He kep' raisin' the devil for an hour an' finally I went and got him with a ten cent plug o' tobacco. He followed me right over to where his stake and chain was an' stood there. Then I chained him up, an' I ain't never had no trouble wit' an elephant since."

Roxie was always known as a bull elephant, as are all females. She had a baby elephant about three and a half feet high. It was born in captivity and given to Roxie to raise. Baby elephants are known as punks. Roxie was indifferent to the punk, so it became Goosey's duty to look after it. Four times each day he went to the cook house to get a concoction of boiled rice and condensed milk that was a substitute for elephant milk. Though Roxie and the

An Elephant Gets Even

punk were advertised as mother and baby, it was really Goosey who mothered the young elephant.

Many of us with the circus felt that Roxie knew of Goosey's affliction. She would touch him in the rear with her trunk at the most unexpected times.

Bill Gleason had been Roxie's trainer for a short period. Roxie always hated him. Whenever he came near her she would raise her trunk and hit the ground until it sounded as though someone had dropped a bass drum. Gleason was always teasing Goosey.

One day as Goosey leaned over to fasten Roxie's leg chain, Gleason touched him in the rear unexpectedly. Goosey carried a bull hook at the time (an ash stick about three feet long with a hook on the end which is used to make the elephant mind by prodding his sensitive skin). He leaped high in the air and brought the bull hook down on Roxie's trunk with great violence. Roxie had seen Gleason running away and laughing. She wheeled quickly and ran after him with a terrible trumpet roar. Gleason saw Roxie running after him and hurried toward the menagerie. That place was in an unroar. Roxie in her speed hit a quarter pole and it crashed on top of the lions' cage. They roared loudly and the noise was taken up by other animals. Gleason ducked out through the sidewall of the tent and Roxie followed him with half the tent draped about her. Goosey hurried after the elephant, and hit her on the trunk with the bull hook. She looked at her friend in pained surprise. As Goosey stood and debated with her, Cameron and Finnerty came up. Cameron ordered Goosey to bring the other two bulls up to Roxie. She was yoked to them and led to place and staked down on all four corners. Then the circus owner ordered Goosey to beat Roxie. He had the spunk to refuse. Cameron started rapping Roxie on her toes, and then gave her a more terrible beating. Her trumpeting could be heard for a far distance. When the beating was over and Cameron had gone, Goosey made up to Roxie by rubbing her behind the ears and feeding her tobacco. As he did so, Gleason foolishly drew near again.

At any rate, Gleason stood within a few feet of Goosey after he had just released Roxie. Roxie watched Gleason with her little pig-like eyes while Goosey picked up a bull hook.

It may have been accidental, but the old circus men said the next move had been deliberately and quickly thought out by Roxie. Goosey's back was turned to Roxie so as to be able to protect himself from Gleason again. But he did not reckon on Roxie.

An Elephant Gets Even

She reached out her trunk and touched Goosey on a sensitive spot. Goosey jumped in the air and yelled and yelled and at the same time brought his bull hook down on Gleason's head as if he were driving a stake.

Gleason fell to the ground with a deep dent in his skull.

Roxie waved her trunk indifferently. The doctor sewed seven stitches in Gleason's head. The show left town without him.

Goosey was not molested again that season.

XIV: A Negro Girl

XIV: A Negro Girl

HE joined us in a Florida town. He was not a typical circus roughneck in appearance. His hair was a wavy black turned prematurely grey. His eyes were deep brown, his jaw was firm, his lips tight, and his body large, well shaped, and muscular.

"Any work here?" he asked Silver Moon Dugan.

"Nope. All filled up. But the property boss needs a man," was the terse reply.

The property boss gave him a sixteen-pound sledge and told him to drive tent stakes. It was before breakfast. By the time the meal was announced he had driven, with the help of two other men, over a hundred stakes to hold the property tent.

He unloaded property effects belonging to performers. He also wore a bright red and green uniform and led a group of Shetland ponies inside the big top when the special act was on.

As Sunday was wash day with the circus, he would always take time to wash his rough clothing.

He worked hard. He smoked a twisted pipe when

sitting alone, and acted disdainful of everybody, including Cameron. We called him "Blackie" among ourselves.

It was not long before we looked upon him as a superior being. His good looks, his strong and clean body, his proud manner fascinated us. We respected his disdain.

He seldom talked to us. When he did, his speech was direct and brutal.

Having created an air of mystery about himself, we were always anxious to learn something about him.

Silver Moon Dugan soon heard of his ability to swing a heavy sledge. He induced him to leave the property boss and join his unit at ten dollars a month increase, or forty dollars a month, top wages on the canvas crew.

He made the change with no more concern than he took in filling his pipe. The stakes were always laid out for him when the tent was to go up. Once the stake was started in the ground by his two helpers he would slam it downward in nine strokes. The sledge would swing upward, the steel glistening in the sun. After making a circle at least eight feet it would hit the stake squarely. No other man with the circus could drive a stake in the ground with less than twelve strokes.

Even Silver Moon Dugan respected him.

"Where you from, Buddy? Been troupin' long?" he asked him.

"Sure thing. I was raised with a circus. My father was Barnum's mother."

Silver Moon Dugan muttered contemptuously to Buddy Conroy, "Funny guy," and let him alone afterward.

"What do you think of Blackie?" I asked Jock.

"You *git* it, say it yourself, kid. He's no regular circus stiff. Look at that nose and that jaw and those eyes that cut like steel. He's got razors in 'em. He was born to be hanged." Jock would say no more.

We left Pensacola, Florida, and played a small town about eighty miles distant. It had drizzled all day and the lot was slippery. Blackie had a habit of walking around it, head bent low, left hand holding the pipe in his mouth.

It was about seven in the evening and the drizzly day lingered faintly. Blackie saw a form in the semi-darkness. "Here—what are you doing there?" he asked quickly.

A scared Negro girl, not over fourteen, had been

trying to crawl under the tent. She stood before him.

"I doan do nothin', jist a peerin' in," she answered, with a half petulant smile.

She was more yellow than black. Her face was beautiful and round, her mouth small, her teeth even and white, her lips full and she was dark-eyed. She wore a plaid dress which curved above her hips and accentuated her lithe and lovely form.

Blackie held her shoulders in his immense hands.

"*God damn*, but you're nice," he said, "slender and clean like a new whip. GOD DAMN!" He crushed her to him.

Pushing her away at arm's-length, he still held her shoulders and looked in her eyes.

"Why in the hell you should have to sneak in a circus is what I'd like to know."

The girl looked up at him with wide eyes of wonder. He put his arm about her. She clung to him at once and pulled his head down and kissed him.

Blackie's eyes blazed. He led the slender young girl, now all animal herself, to the rear of the snake-charmer's wagon. She was heard to cry, "Oh Misteh Man, Misteh Man," a few times as if in pain. Then all became very still.

Later, he put her on a mattress in an empty

A Negro Girl

canvas-covered wagon and stood guard over it while fifteen white circus roughnecks entered one at a time. Before entering, each man gave Blackie a half dollar.

When the last man had gone Blackie smuggled the girl into the big top.

Late that night, as the circus train was ready to pull out, the little Negro girl saw Blackie standing in the open door of a car.

Running with arms extended she yelled, "Misteh Man, Misteh Man!" and tried to board the car as the train started.

We watched Blackie's unchanging expression. The girl held desperately to the car and tried to swing her lithe body inside. "Let her come on in," yelled Silver Moon Dugan.

"*What?* A nigger wench?" snapped Blackie as he put his foot against the girl's forehead and kicked her from the car.

The girl could be heard wailing pitifully above the accumulating noise of the rolling cars, "Misteh Man, Misteh—Man—do come on back, Misteh Man!"

The engine whistle shrieked as we rattled by red and green lights.

*   *   *

Circus Parade

No man spoke for a long time. I watched their changing expressions. Silver Moon Dugan's eyes looked a trifle sad. I heard Blackie trying to puff his pipe. It had gone out. He remained silent for some minutes. He then lit a match and smoked.

XV: Red-Lighted

XV: Red-Lighted

SILVER MOON DUGAN was known as the greatest "red-lighter" in the country. Red-lighting was an ancient and dishonorable custom indulged in by many a circus twenty years ago.

The act consisted of opening the side door of a moving car, and kicking the undesirable traveler out.

How the term originated is in confusion. Some ruffian authorities claimed that men were only kicked off trains near the red lights of a railroad yard. But I have seen many kicked off circus trains where no red lights gleamed at all.

But there can be no doubt that the practice originated in order to cheat circus laborers and other roustabouts out of their wages. If the victim persisted in walking many miles and following the circus he was chased off the lot. There was no redress in any of the states for those cheated. The poor man's justice then, as now, was not only blind, but lame and halt.

Silver Moon Dugan had been with Cameron's World's Greatest Combined Shows three years. He

Circus Parade

was either of French or Spanish extraction. How he came by any of his names no one ever knew. He was tall, wiry and dark. He had thin straggly hair. His black eyes burned out of a rat face. He had a club foot and walked with a limp. He could talk French, Italian, German, and excellent English when necessary.

His greeting each morning to his roughneck canvasmen was, "Good morning, sons. You know what kinda sons I mean."

Dugan was nearly aways drunk, but never showed it. He was a hard, domineering, brutal, snarling driver of men. He carried a blackjack and a revolver at all times. He could load or unload a circus faster, and with fewer men, than any other canvas boss in the nation.

To mark a lot for a tent it is necessary to make accurate measurements. A steel tape is used to locate places for centre poles, dressing tents and stakes.

Silver Moon Dugan could walk on a lot, give it a quick glance as he limped about on his club foot, and know with unerring precision in five minutes just how the tent was to be placed. "You gotta know your canvas," he would say as he would allow two feet for shrinkage if the tent was wet. If the canvas

[230]

was extremely dry, he would allow for its stretching a foot.

Once on the lot, he would gather a bundle of "laying out pins," wire needles about a quarter of an inch in diameter and two feet long. The eyes of the needles were about an inch in circumference. To each was tied a piece of red flannel. Dugan would throw these needles in the ground with exact precision at the point where a stake was to be driven.

A canvas boss of the old school, he hated all advance men, those fellows who traveled ahead of the circus. He blamed them for rough lots, inclement weather, poor business and bad food.

Once while hurrying about the lot he stumbled over a pile of manure. "The God damn advance man's fault," he yelled, unmindful of the fact that the advance man had no control over local horses.

Two men had been his lieutenants during the years he spent with Cameron. One was Gorilla Haley, so named because he looked like a gorilla and moved slower than the sands of time.

The other man was called "The Ghost." He was more like shadow than reality, a shambling watery man with uneven shoulders, a crooked mouth and a hare lip. He was a man who never did anything right. Clumsy and filthy, a human nearly as low in the mental scale as an animal, he worshipped Silver Moon Dugan as a god. That was his chief value in the world. Dugan had carried "The Ghost" with one circus or another for eleven years.

Dugan never smiled. The right corner of his mouth would merely twist in a leer when he was amused. Judging him from the memory of adolescence, I am certain he had no sense of humor. Rather did he have a sense of the atrociously ridiculous. The right corner of his mouth was seen to twist several times when he heard Goosey hitting Gleason with the bull hook.

Dugan hired many romantic young men who wished to see the world. "I'll show 'em the world," he used to say, "at the end of a sledge."

Two weeks before he had come across a young fellow who was anxious to travel. Dugan observed his clothes and watch. He agreed to give the young man twenty-five dollars per week and a chance "to work himself up," after he discovered he could bring a few hundred dollars with him.

He told the young fellow, who was a railroader, that it would be necessary to bring a good watch so as to be on time for work each morning. "Promptness is a jewel," were his words. He also told him to bring several suits, two pairs of shoes, a good pistol and all the money possible, as the first month's salary was held back.

The youth reported to Dugan with two suitcases full of clothes, three hundred dollars in money and an expensive watch. The next day Dugan told him to put on overalls and save his good clothes for the larger towns. Clothes, watch and money were left in Dugan's care.

The young fellow was now huddled in the car with Dugan, Blackie, The Ghost, Gorilla Haley, myself and several others.

At the next stop, Cameron and Slug Finnerty crawled into the car and talked over details of the next day with Silver Moon Dugan. The train started before they could get off and go to their own section.

"It's only a sixty-mile run now to ——, and not a stop. We'll make it in a couple of hours," said Silver Moon as Cameron and Finnerty resigned themselves to their environment.

The rain rattled heavily on the roof of the car. The late season was making business even poorer. Everyone was in an evil mood.

The heavy sopping pieces of canvas had been rolled into huge bundles and put at one end of the

Circus Parade

car. "We've paraffined 'em till they cracks but they don't hold off water no more. It soaks right through," said Dugan to Cameron.

The car was lighted with smoky kerosene lamps such as were used in old-fashioned railway cars. The kerosene smoke, the odor of bad liquor and filthy bodies, the reek of the wet and muddy canvas filled the air. Combined with the rainy and gloomy night it all seemed unreal to my tired brain, the haunted fragment of an ugly dream. A few men played cards with a dirty deck. The Ghost smoked the butts of cigars he had collected under the seats in the big tent after the show.

There were no bunks in the car. Every canvasman slept in a dirty blanket in wet weather, or on the rolls of canvas in hot, in any spot which he could keep hold by right of might.

The romance of circus life had fast faded from the young fellow as he looked for a spot upon which to stretch his shivering body. No man talked. We lay like stunned animals on soggy ground. The young man had seen neither clothes, money nor watch since joining the show.

He looked about at the dreary assemblage and then looked up at the roof upon which the rain pounded heavily.

Red-Lighted

"Gee, I wish I had a nice clean bed and a warm bath," he whined. The card players paused for a moment and frowned at the boy. The Ghost held the butt of his cigar and looked at the young fellow a moment, then put the bad-smelling tobacco rope in his mouth and resumed gazing at his feet. Blackie held his pipe tightly.

I looked across the car at him and wondered. He was not one of us. But what was he? He made of silence a drama.

He now rubbed his beaked nose with the stem of his crooked pipe. Gorilla Haley, with arms spread out, snored like a grand opera singer. Silver Moon Dugan lay on a roll of dry flags of many nations. They had not been used on the main tent that day on account of rain. He breathed heavily with asthma.

Cameron and Finnerty, oblivious of surroundings, sat on a bundle of wet canvas and talked.

The old car rattled, swayed and creaked over the rough roadbed. Thick sprays of rain blew in through the cracks of the side doors.

Silver Moon Dugan buttoned his red flannel shirt and, rising to his feet, made his way quickly over piles of canvas and stacks of poles and seats.

Accustomed to dirt, and the squalor of the cir-

Circus Parade

cus, the corner of his mouth twisted at the young fellow's desire for a bed and a bath.

He put his hand on the boy's shoulder.

"So it's a bath and a bed you want, my lad," he said, not unkindly, as he opened the door about two feet. "See if you can see any red lights ahead." The young fellow looked out and answered, "No."

"All right," jeered Dugan, "there's a nice road-bed down there, an' a whole damn sky full of bath." He kicked the young adventure searcher out of the car.

XVI: Surprise

XVI: Surprise

NO man moved. The boss canvasman pushed the door shut quickly. Cameron and Finnerty, momentarily disturbed, resumed talking. The card players were soon quarreling again over the game.

"I took it with my ace," insisted one.

"You did like hell, you mean you took an ace from underneath," scowled the other.

Silver Moon Dugan joined Cameron and Finnerty.

Gorilla Haley rose, his jaws swollen with tobacco juice. He rushed to the door and swung it open.

"God Almighty, Gorilla, it's wet enough outside. Do you wanta flood the state?" the Ghost asked.

"Shut your trap," flared Gorilla, shambling back to his place.

My worn brain would not allow me to sleep.

I thought once of crawling over the train to the horse car. One of the horses had been ill that day and I knew that Jock would travel with him. It suddenly dawned on me that the car had no end exits, out of which I might have muscled myself onto the roof of the next car.

Blackie, still holding his pipe, rose indifferently and walked to the end of the car. He stood still for a moment, legs spread apart, head down. In another second he laid his pipe on a wet piece of canvas, then turned, facing us.

"Everybody stand up!" He whipped out the words sharply. In his extended right hand a blue steel gun. It looked to me as long as a railroad tie.

We all rose like soldiers standing at attention. Cameron was the most obedient. Silver Moon hesitated.

"Work fast, you lame bastard. I just want an excuse to send you to hell." He took one step forward. "I'll put a hole through you so big you can pound a stake in it." Silver Moon's lip curled, as he hesitated about putting up his hands.

For a paralyzing second I thought Blackie would shoot. He held the gun on a level with Dugan's heart and moved nearer. I closed my eyes as if to shut out the noise of the explosion. Then Blackie's voice went on. "What a dirty bunch of sons of bitches you all are." Then, looking straight at Dugan, Cameron and Finnerty—"Throw your gats down. And let me hear them fall hard. Come on."

[240]

Surprise

Finnerty and Dugan threw revolvers on the floor.

"Now throw your money down—fast—every God damn one of you." Pocketbooks followed the guns. I threw a twenty-five cent piece.

Blackie half-grinned as it lit near a revolver.

He turned to me. "Open that door, kid." Obedient at once, I slid the door backward its full length of six feet.

The noise of the rushing train increased. The rain swished across the car.

"Now everybody turn around. Walk to the door —and *jump*. The guy that turns gets a bullet through his dome."

Cameron looked at Blackie appealingly. Blackie laughed.

"You crooked old hypocrite, you can't talk your way outta this." He lunged forward with the gun and shouted, "JUMP!"

Being second to no man in the art of catching a flying train, I jumped swiftly and with supreme confidence. The rest of the men followed me.

Before I could gain my balance on the soggy ground, a car had passed. There were two more to come. I knew every iron ladder and every portion of the train by heart. I could see the forms of the other men, some stretched out, others scrambling to their feet on the ground. I heard an unearthly screech. A gun went off.

My brain, long trained in hobo lore, functioned fast. I sized up the ground to make sure of my footing and looked ahead to make sure I would crash into no bridge while running swiftly with the train.

When one more car whirled by me, I started running.

If I missed the end of the last car I at least would not be thrown under the train. Running full speed, my brain racing with my feet, I knew that to grab was one thing, to grab and not to miss was another, and to cling like frozen death once my hands went round the iron rung of the ladder. I knew that I must race with the train, else if I grabbed it while I stood still, my arms might be jerked out of their sockets.

My cap was gone. The rain slashed across my face. When about to grab, my right foot slipped, and I was thrown off my balance for a second.

With muscles suddenly taut, then loosened like a springing tiger's, I sprang upward. My hands clung to the iron rung. My body was jerked toward the train. Thinking quickly, I buried my jaw in my left shoulder, pugilist fashion. It saved me from

[242]

Surprise

being knocked out by the impact of my jaw with the side of the car. I finally got my left foot on the bottom of the ladder, my right leg dangling.

The car passed the group who had been redlighted with me. A man grabbed at my right foot. I kicked desperately, and felt for an instant my foot against the flesh of his face. My arms ached as though they were being severed from my shoulders with a razor blade. A numbness crept over me. My brain throbbed in unison with my heart. Drilled in primitive endurance of the road for four long years, I was to face the supreme test.

I had no love for the red-lighted men. Rather, I admired Blackie more. Neither did I blame him for red-lighting me. A man had once trusted another in my world. He was betrayed.

I had the young road kid's terrible aversion against walking the track for any man. My law was —to stay with the train, to allow no man to "ditch" me.

When the numbness left me I crawled up the ladder. Blinded by the rain, my hair plastered to my head in spite of the wind that roared round the train, I lay, face downward, and clawed with tired hands at the roof of the smooth wet car.

Circus Parade

Sometime afterward, whether a minute or an hour, I do not know, I tried to rise. My arms bent. I lay flat again.

My mania had been to tell Jock. It suddenly dawned on me to tell anybody I saw. But how could I see anyone while the train lurched through the wind-driven and rain-washed night?

I cried in the intensity of emotion. Pulling myself together, I dragged my body to the end of the first car, about sixty feet. Reaching there, I had not the strength to muscle my body to the next car. After a seemingly endless exertion I pulled myself across the three-foot chasm between the two cars. Beneath me the wheels clicked with fierce revolutions on the rails. The wind blew the rain in heavy gusts through the chasm.

With the aid of the chain which ran from the wheel at the top of the car to the brake beneath, I worked my body around to the ladder, and crawled laboriously to the top of the second car. My muscles throbbed with pain at the armpits. I wondered if I had dislocated my arms. I tried to crawl on my hands and knees, and gave it up. Finally I succeeded in dragging myself across the second car. My heart pounded as though it would jump from my breast.

[244]

Surprise

I leaned out from my position between the cars. The light still gleamed in the open door of the car from which we had been red-lighted.

Blackie was standing in the doorway. His shadow was thrown far across the ground. The running train gave it a weird dancing effect. It pumped over the rough earth and cut through telegraph poles and fences as the rain splashed upon it.

The engine whistled loud and long. My heart jumped with glee. It was going to stop. Suddenly the train gained momentum and the engine whistled twice. This meant: straight through. We passed a few red and green lights, and later some that were yellowish white.

The whistle shrieked again, a low moaning dismal effort like a whistle being blown under water. I sensed a long run for the train. The fireman's hand lay heavily on the bell rope. It became light as day each time he opened the fire-box to shovel in coal.

The rain still slashed downward with blinding fury. In spite of everything my eyes became heavy. Knowing the folly of going to sleep and falling between the cars, I opened my coat and held my body close to the iron rod which held the brake. I then buttoned the coat around it. While being forced to stand as rigid as one in a straight jacket, it would nevertheless save me from being dashed under the wheels.

After many wet miles the train slowed at the edge of a railroad yard. Lights from engines blended with white steam and made the yards light as early day.

I looked across the yards and saw Blackie making for the open road.

We gained speed for a few minutes and then ran slower, at last coming to a stop in the yards.

I hurried to the horse car and found Jock. He was sitting on some straw near Jerry, the sick horse. I gasped out the story of the red-lighting to him.

Jock said without energy, "It was a tough break for you, kid," and shrugged his shoulders. "I'll tell the Baby Buzzard." He frowned. "We'll have to go back after them, I guess."

He studied for another moment. "It would be a great stunt to let 'em walk in. They deserve it. *But no.* I guess it's best for you to come and tell the Baby Buzzard. We'll be all finished in a week and you'd lose your wages if you ducked now and didn't tell."

"Yeah, Jock, you're right," I said. And then, "I saw Blackie beatin' it across the yards about a mile back."

"Well," exclaimed Jock, "say nothin' about it,

kid. A guy that kin pull a stunt like that deserves to go free. I don't think he meant you no harm. He *had* to red-light you, too."

"Gosh! I wonder what he'd think if he knew I made the train again."

"He wouldn't be surprised. He'd have made it if you'd of red-lighted him. He's just a hell of a guy, that's all."

Jock put on his soft grease-stained hat. "We'd better go an' tell the Baby Buzzard together, kid, but don't mention seein' Blackie. Let him make his getaway. I wouldn't turn a dog over to the law."

"All right, Jock," I muttered, and followed him out of the car.

XVII: A Railroad Order

XVII: A Railroad Order

THE misty morning at last turned clear. The sun shone bright. We walked toward the Baby Buzzard's car. In a few words I told my story. The Baby Buzzard's eyes narrowed.

"Who'd you say red-lighted 'em?"

I told her again.

"What become of him?" she asked.

"That don't matter," answered Jock, "it's what'll become of them if we don't get 'em. Maybe they're hurt, or even killed."

The Baby Buzzard sneered. "Killed hell. No sich luck for some of 'em." Then quickly, "Come with me."

We followed her toward the engine. The fireman leaned out of the left window and watched the engineer oil the large drive wheels.

The Baby Buzzard approached him and asked, "Are you a runnin' this here train?"

"I was, till it stopped," he answered with irritation.

The engineer's answer angered the Baby Buzzard.

Circus Parade

"Well, would you mind runnin' your damn train back about fifty mile an' pickin' up my husban' and some more of his men that got red-lighted with the kid here."

"Not me, lady. I'm all through. I've been smellin' this circus long enough. You'll have to tell your troubles to the trainmaster. He's right over in that corner of the round house."

We walked across the tracks in the direction of the round house, a place in which the engines were kept like so many automobiles in a huge round garage. The Baby Buzzard hobbled along with us, delivering a scathing remark toward the engineer, which ran, "The nerve o' that devil. No wonder poor people git no wheres in this world. They're too damn saucy."

The trainmaster had one arm and a happy smile. His hair was sandy, his face the color of an over-ripe mulberry. He telephoned the chief train despatcher and asked, "What's due out of ——? Boss of the circus and some other fellows made to walk the plank."

Turning to me—"You say it was about fifty miles out? No towns between of any size?"

"No sir."

The despatcher made answer!

A Railroad Order

"Then Number Four'll ketch 'em if they've stayed close to the track. All right—tell conductor Number Four to be on lookout for them—bring 'em on in here."

"How long'll it be?"

"About three or four hours, lady."

The Baby Buzzard grunted and walked away. "Pay the railroads all the damn money you make an' then they can't do you a little favor. Have to wait all this time to git started."

The Baby Buzzard lost no time in getting the circus unloaded. The property boss was given Silver Moon Dugan's work to do. Buddy Conroy took charge in place of Slug Finnerty.

She hobbled about snapping orders. The men cursed her under their breath.

An old "roughneck" canvasman and stake-driver laid out the tent on the lot. And to the surprise of all it was done as well as Dugan could have accomplished.

Jock gave me some dry clothes and allowed me to sleep until time for the parade to return. All that day I basked in my little glory.

Number Four arrived after dinner with its diversified cargo.

Cameron with both legs broken, was carried out

Circus Parade

of the caboose. On his face was scorn for his position and pity for himself.

The entire circus gathered about the train. Silver Moon Dugan looked ashamed. His limp was more decided.

"How's hittin' the ties, Silver?" yelled a voice.

"Go to hell," was Silver's retort.

The Ghost and Gorilla Halen were unhurt.

Back of them came the young fellow whom Silver Moon Dugan had red-lighted.

His clothing was badly torn, his face deeply scratched.

As I had spread the story of his first having been red-lighted by Dugan, his appearance was greeted with a wild shout.

A doctor was called. He pulled and twisted at Cameron's legs, and then put them in crude plaster casts. The battered barbarian looked at them when the doctor had finished. He glanced then at the Baby Buzzard and shook his head violently, at last snapping out:

"God damn the God damned luck!"

One of the hardest, the most merciless, and the meanest of mankind, who had red-lighted many men himself and who had cheated many hundreds in his wandering life, he added:

[254]

A Railroad Order

"That man ain't human. He's lower'n a skunk's belly."

"Well he's hard enough to be human," sneered Silver Moon Dugan, "and I've seen him somewhere. It seems to me he pulled a fast one with Robinson's five or six years ago. Believe me or not, if I ever put my glims on 'im agin there'll be music along this railroad. I'll play 'Home Sweet Home' on his God damn ribs with bullets."

Cameron tried to turn over. His body twitched with pain.

"You're a tune too late, Silver. You'll never see that bozo this side of hell." His eyes were bleared with the wind and rain of the night. They were crossed for a moment with clouds of humor.

"But you gotta say this, Silver, you done met your match in that greaser."

"I have like so much hell," returned Silver Moon Dugan.

Cameron, oblivious of the retort, added:

"It's funny about people. The minute I saw that guy I felt like apologizin' for ownin' the show. That's the kind of a guy he was. His damn hard eyes were like diamond drills an' his nose hooked like a buzzard's. He's no regular roughneck, I knew it, but what'n hell is he?"

Circus Parade

The Baby Buzzard, never soft, looked down at the hulk with broken legs. She started to say something, changed her mind, then turned to me. Her flat and aged breast rose once, then sank. An emotion was killed within her.

In all the months she displayed no interest in me, save that I could read well aloud—and now:

"Where you from, kid?"

"Oh, I'm just a drifter. Joined on in Louisiana before the Lion Tamer got bumped off."

"That's right. I'd forgot," she returned. "Did that lousy wretch take your money too?"

"My last two bits," I replied.

The Baby Buzzard allowed herself the shadow of a grin. Then for fear of being too generous with herself, she frowned.

"Damn his hide, the nerve. A guy that'd do that ud skin a louse for its hide."

She handed me a half dollar. Clutching it in my hand I returned to Jock.

Cameron insisted on being present each time the tent was pitched. A covered wagon was turned over to him, the canvas on each side being made to roll up like curtains. It was roped off from the gaze of the public. Here he would lie like a flabby, wounded but unbeaten general directing his forces. I was his errand boy.

The circus was to close in a week. The nights even in the South were now cold. Frost covered everything each morning. Roughnecks, musicians, acrobats, all talked of a headquarters for the winter.

Cameron's reputation as a red-lighter had been accentuated by his own catastrophe. "He'll have to pay us now, the old devil. He can't make a gitaway on broken pins," was the comment of the old roughneck who had laid out the tents in Silver Moon Dugan's absence.

But nevertheless we were all worried about our wages. If we allowed the show to go into headquarters in another state it would be impossible to collect. We would not be allowed to go near Cameron's headquarters. Citizens and police would protect Cameron against the claims of circus hoboes. Such communities had always protected Cameron and his tribe of red-lighting circus owners from the ravages of roughnecks who wanted justice.

I could feel the tension on the lot. Many of the older canvasmen had what is known as a "month's holdback" due them, twenty or thirty dollars for a month of drudging labor. It was wealth to men of

Circus Parade

our kind to whom a dollar was often opulence.

The final pay-day would cost Cameron several thousand dollars. How would he face the situation with two broken legs? We all wondered.

"You'll git yours, kid, don't worry," Jock had assured me. But even then, I was not so sure.

To ease my mind I talked over the matter indirectly with the Baby Buzzard.

"Gosh, I'll feel rich next Thursday, when the show closes," I said to her.

"What for?" she asked. "Money only runes people like you. You won't do nothin' with it but git drunk an' go to whore houses an' git your backbones weak."

I passed the word along. It made us more determined to collect than ever.

XVIII: The Last Day

XVIII: The Last Day

PUTTING up the tent was a spasmodic effort on the last day.

A feeling of uneasiness pervaded the lot. A half dozen roughnecks rejoined us. They had deserted the show after the hey rube fight.

"What? You back?" roared Silver Moon Dugan, as they advanced in a body toward him.

"Yeap, what's left of us, Silver," the ringleader replied insolently. "An' we want our dough, too. This is pay day, you know."

Dugan parleyed with them no more. They either looked too formidable, or he had other plans. No attempt was made to "chase 'em off the lot."

Instead, Dugan hurried to Cameron. They were soon joined by Finnerty, Jock and the Baby Buzzard. I went with Jock.

Jock's heart was never with Cameron. He loved morphine and horses. Life was to him, except when he had "a habit on," a dream that had broken in the middle and had left him dazed. Every horse had his love. He was all pity when he saw a galled

Circus Parade

shoulder or spavin on any animal, whether it were in his keeping or not.

The "paste brigade" awaited our arrival. Traveling days ahead of us in the advance car, they were now ready to go into winter headquarters with buckets, paste and several unused tons of vari-colored circus advertising.

Giant yellow, red and green posters everywhere announced Cameron's "acres of tents."

The paste brigade and other advance men left in their car at noon after a long parley with Cameron.

One of the paste slingers waved some greenbacks at us.

It made us more hopeful of being paid that day.

Word was soon spread that we were to be given our wages next day at Cameron's winter headquarters. A feeling of rebellion followed.

Silver Moon Dugan exerted himself to keep his canvasmen from mixing with their six former comrades. To avoid open warfare he used all the crude diplomacy of which he was capable.

He realized that if the local police were called in there would be a great deal of damage done. Another general hey rube fight might result.

By an underground current the workingmen had

The Last Day

decided that Cameron was to pay or the circus would not move.

Cameron's legs were heavily plastered and held high above his head with a rope and pulley. In spite of this he was half propped up in his bed when we arrived.

The canvas curtains were down on each side of the wagon. The Baby Buzzard rose when I entered. Her manner was very kind. I sensed what was to follow.

Presently Goosey and the property boss entered. There was much random talk of the situation, then Jock's voice:

"Don't try it, I'm tellin' you, you'll never move the show."

"Well we can't pay 'em here. We've got to figger things up an' it'll take till tomorrow to do it," said Finnerty.

Jock interrupted with, "Well it's no skin off my beak, but I've gotta play half-square. All I'm tellin' you is—*don't*."

"Well, the boss has a right to pay tomorrow if he likes," snapped Silver Moon Dugan. "You'll have the dough for your bunch. That'll let you out."

"But it won't let you fellows out," Jock looked down at Cameron. Finnerty rubbed his one eye.

Circus Parade

"Oh hell," he said, "tell 'em to come to winter headquarters for their money. Who gives a damn about a lot of hoboes, anyhow. Money spoils bums, that's my opinion."

"Same here," snapped the Baby Buzzard.

Cameron motioned to me.

"Here, kid, take this message to the men. Just tell 'em I said pay-day was tomorrow. At two o'clock every man will get his bonus and we'll have a big barbecue in the evening."

Jock followed me out. Together we walked in the direction of the horses. There was a blare of music along the midway.

A strong wind began to blow. Tiny pieces of paper and empty peanut sacks whirled about the lot. Jock said nothing to me. He walked slowly, and save for a nervous twitching about the mouth was calm.

"We'll go tell 'em, kid," he said at last, "but tell 'em I got the money for my squad today. You should worry, you'll never want to travel with this damned outfit again anyhow. This is goin' to be the damndest blow-off Cameron ever had. I can feel it in the air."

The men received Cameron's message with sullen contempt. They stood in groups about the lot.

When the last rube had gone home, and while

The Last Day

the wind swirled across the lot carrying the debris of a rustic holiday with it, at least a hundred and fifty men marched toward Cameron's wagon.

Down the midway they came, Rosebud Bates in the lead playing on the clarinet.

There'll be a hot time in the old town tonight.

Back of Rosebud Bates was Blackie.

His appearance startled me. I could hardly believe my eyes.

"I knew he'd show up again, by God," said Jock. Blackie's eyes were wild in his face.

"Is he drunk?" I asked Jock.

"Nope. He's full o' heroin."

The six roughnecks who had appeared early were with him, three on each side. Their eyes, less vivid, still had something of the same expression as Blackie's. Each of their right hands were in their right coat pockets. Their coats were jerked sideways as their arms swung. Blackie's coat was unbuttoned. Experience had taught me that the hands gripped revolvers in the coat pockets. If trouble came, the bullets would rip through the cloth.

They marched directly to Cameron's wagon.

"Good Lord, Jock, what'll happen?" I asked.

Circus Parade

"Anything. When guys are loaded up on heroin it'll give 'em more nerve an' make 'em more desperate an' make 'em think faster'n anything on earth." He grunted. "Cameron's in trouble sure as hell. I just know now that Blackie was loaded when he red-lighted you guys."

A shot was fired from the rear of the wagon. Blackie, untouched, started running toward it. The others followed him.

Silver Moon Dugan and Finnerty stood near the rear wheel.

"Thought you'd git me quick, did you, Silver," sneered Blackie, hand held high in his coat pocket. Dugan hesitated, his mind not as alert as Blackie's who was on fire with murderous heroin.

Blackie fired. The bullet crashed through the thick muscle of Dugan's right arm.

He groaned dismally. The gun dropped. One of Blackie's comrades picked it up.

Blackie then stepped in close. His immense arm went upward. There followed a bone-crushing thud. Dugan's jaw cracked. He sank.

Finnerty, dumbfounded by the suddenness of Blackie's action, held his hands up as if to plead. Blackie sprang at him with the agility of a mountain panther.

[266]

The Last Day

His hand left his pocket, clinging to his blue revolver. Half circling, he twisted Finnerty's body until it seemed he would break his back. Then his monstrous arm went around Finnerty's throat like a vise.

"Search the rat. Quick," he yelled.

Two men pounced upon Finnerty ripped a watch and chain from his breast and went through his pockets swiftly. In another instant Blackie's gun thudded brutally against his jaw. It tore Finnerty's flesh and covered his one good eye with blood.

The men surrounded the wagon. "Keep a gun on these birds," snapped Blackie. A roughneck stood over the unconscious Finnerty and Dugan.

Gorilla Haley and four others of Dugan's henchmen ran quickly toward the wagon. They were caught like mice in a trap.

Blackie saw them and yelled, *"Hey Rube!* Dugan's stool pigeons! Let 'em have it!"

Cameron lay in his bed helpless while the Baby Buzzard shrieked curses.

"Ain't they a man among you, you God damn crummy varmints."

Her shrieks were soon lost in the avalanche of brutality that followed.

[267]

Circus Parade

The "Ghost" collapsed in fear before a fist reached him.

"Give him the boot," yelled Blackie. His face and body were quickly kicked beyond recognition.

He squirmed on the ground like a mass of blubber and then became rigid.

The rest were annihilated by more than a hundred circus roughnecks, a tribe of men the equal of which in sheer courage and primitive fighting ability no frontier country in the world's history has ever produced.

Recruited from the roughest of the rough, surviving hunger, cold, dreary and seemingly endless hours of labor without fatigue, they were now in their proper element.

Gorilla Haley, the seasoned fighter, did immediately that which had made his name a byword in annals of circus barbarism. He looked about quickly and backed against the wagon so that no one could get behind him. He would at least be able to see his antagonists.

"He'll get it anyhow," said Jock, "the damn fool. It's not his circus. They'll murder him."

Gorilla Haley was everything in the human calendar of vices. But he was not a coward.

Weighing at least two hundred and forty pounds

The Last Day

of muscles, his immense sparse body bent low, his long arms reached out with fierce blows and warded off the attacks of a dozen men. Blackie shouted, "Lay off, men, I'll give him a chance and take him myself."

The wind had died down for a few moments. Combined with the temporary lull of voices, the effect was spectral.

The mind even in great danger often sees pictures for an instant that are remembered a lifetime. I threw my head back from sheer fatigue of excitement.

Above me was a deep blue sky dotted with shining regiments of wonder. An immense silver and blue cloud seemed hung suspended in the center of the blue dome.

Tired and wretched at the end of a long season of migratory labor, with nothing but the insecurity of a gypsy at the finish, I still had left that mightiest heritage of toil-worn men—a sense of wonder.

To the left was the Milky Way. A half Pawnee Indian stake-driver, long since red-lighted, had told me one night as our train traveled through an edge of Kansas that the Milky Way was only white dust made by a horse ten miles high and a buffalo even taller, racing like hell and high water across the

Circus Parade

sky. He told me that the horse ran on one side where the biggest stars were; that the buffalo made the little dust.

Reality blotted out the sky. The lull ended.

Blackie, not so ponderous as Gorilla Haley, closed in upon him as we formed a ring around them. Never was there fiercer impact. Their foreheads crashed together. Stunned, Gorilla's knees sagged. Blackie's wild eyes danced like a vicious animal's. He tore the clothing from Gorilla's body as he yelled, "I like to fight 'em naked."

The cloud darkened and ran down the sky on all sides like spilled ink. The wind came up. It thundered. Rain drops rattled on the paper-strewn ground.

Into the fusillade of blows Blackie stepped. One caught him across the nose and the blood streamed. Angered to a pitch of even fiercer fury, he struck with accurate aim at Gorilla's head and body.

With clothing torn from their bodies they cursed each other through lacerated lips. They broke apart and crashed together again. Breasts heaving, faces trickling blood, they reeled, punch-drunk, under the brain-jarring monotony of blows.

The men pushed in closer and the fighters had barely room in which to move. All of Gorilla's cau-

[270]

The Last Day

tion was not enough. A black jack crashed upon his skull as Blackie's mallet fist connected under his chin. He fell instantly. Blackie kicked him in the face.

One of the six roughnecks rushed up to Blackie. "I done it! I done it!" he shouted.

Blackie looked toward the big top and yelled, *"Hurray!!"*

Instantly the circus grounds were lit like day.

There came the shrill neighing of horses, and the whining of other animals.

"The big top's on fire," shouted the army of roustabouts. Forgetting money, they all ran toward the burning tent.

"Let 'er burn," yelled Blackie as he sprang into Cameron's wagon followed by the six roughnecks.

The curtains of the wagon were ripped off.

"Where's your money, you broken-legged old faker? This is pay-day. I've got three weeks' wages comin'. Do you think I swing a sledge for you for nothing?" And Blackie danced a jig before the prostrate Cameron, saying, "The boobs love a fire. It gets them every time."

Sheets of white and yellow flame crackled upward.

The Baby Buzzard rushed at Blackie, her with-

Circus Parade

ered fists clenched. "Hold this old rip," shouted Blackie.

One of the men grabbed her carelessly. She scratched and bit until he pinioned her arms. Another man held her legs.

Cameron raised his hand. "Won't you listen a moment, gentlemen?"

Then the cry reached his ears, "The main tent's burnin'."

The magnificent old ruffian jerked his plastered legs from their moorings and tried to stand erect.

The crackling flames mingled with the roar of lions and the wails of hyenas. The elephants trumpeted. A panther screamed like a woman.

Cameron stood erect and tried to walk. The seven desperadoes laughed as he fell backward.

Blackie, eyes blazing, stepped close to his cot and slapped his face.

"You don't remember red-lightin' me, do you, you old double crossing bastard? Well, I *do*. And you didn't break my legs neither. But to hell with that. It's money we want. I'm paymaster now. Where's the money?"

Blackie laughed like a maniac. The old man lay silent.

[272]

The Last Day

The noises increased. Men shouted everywhere. The flames brightened.

"The old paraffine tent burns like dry matches," exclaimed an excited canvasman. Cameron heard the words.

A more deathly calm came over him. "Who started the fire?" he asked dully, rubbing his bleared and tired eyes.

"Where's the money?" shouted Blackie.

The circus owner's mouth went tighter still. He glared at Blackie. The seven men edged closer about the cot.

"All right, you won't talk?" Blackie held a gun at Cameron's temple. The broken-legged circus owner's eyes closed as though awaiting a bullet to rip through his head.

Blackie put his left foot forward. His body was tense. Death was five inches from Cameron's brain. Blackie's finger rubbed the trigger.

The Baby Buzzard screamed shrilly, her nerve broken:

"Under his bed. Under his bed."

Blackie withdrew the gun. The cot was pushed to one side. The undaunted Cameron tried to leap upon Blackie as he stooped for the money, secure in heavy sacks in an open safe.

Circus Parade

Blackie threw a heavy fist against Cameron's jaw. His plastered legs spread out. His head went backward. He lay still.

"Now it's pay-day, men." Blackie motioned to the six cronies. "Hold the guns level. If anybody comes near, spatter his brains out."

The Baby Buzzard was tied with a rope and placed by Cameron's side. Blackie then ordered Finnerty and Dugan tied.

The wagon was overturned. The old lady screamed.

"Shut up or we'll burn it," yelled Blackie as he rushed into the darkness followed by the six ruffians.

*   *   *

Silver Moon Dugan regained consciousness and rolled over. The canvasmen returned and stared at the upturned wagon. Cameron and the Baby Buzzard groaned.

The wild confusion at last died down.

Citizens and police, attracted by the fire, now swarmed the lot.

All that was left of the big top were the three charred poles which had once held it. Red remnants of pine seats still glowed.

The gilded circus wagons were turned black with

The Last Day

heat and smoke. The wind blew the odor of burnt paraffine over the circus ground.

The animals paced nervously in their cages. An elephant trumpeted. Two horses neighed; one after the other.

Soon the lot was deserted.

The silence of desolation reigned where the big top once had been.

XIX: Later

XIX: Later

NO trace of Blackie or his comrades could be found. The police asked many questions, and left. The circus roustabouts looked at each other sheepishly.

Silver Moon Dugan was taken to the hospital, his arm shot away.

Gorilla Haley's skull was fractured. He became insane. He later became a member of the Chicago police.

Finnerty, beaten but not broken, took charge of everything. He stood at the end of Cameron's wagon, which had been placed upright again. Cameron, his jaw bandaged, was in a half-sitting position as Finnerty addressed the men:

"We have shared danger together, gentlemen, and now we have endured robbery. It was our intention to pay you each and all, here this evening, but that, alas, cannot now be done.

"But we hold you no ill-will. Your mistake, if any, was of the head rather than of the heart."

As Finnerty continued the men became more shamefaced and uneasy.

Circus Parade

"I will wire our headquarters at Mr. Cameron's suggestion tonight." Cameron, feeling his bandaged jaw, nodded his approval.

"The money to pay each and every one of Cameron's World's Greatest Combined Shows will be here in the morning. I will meet you in front of the post office at eleven tomorrow and pay you. Those who would rather travel on to headquarters may do so."

The circus was loaded with alacrity.

At ten o'clock next morning the men marched in a body toward the post office.

Finnerty left with them. At ten forty-five the circus train departed for winter headquarters.

Finnerty was aboard.

UTTERLY RAFTED

PAULINE MANDERS